Praise for the No

writing as Jessica Bird

"Jessica Bird gives us a romance of rare depth,
humor and sensuality."
—*RT Book Reviews* on *Beauty and the Black Sheep*

"Dramatic, edgy and intense, this story
has a larger-than-life, dark hero who takes the
sweet heroine (and the reader) to some exciting places."
—*RT Book Reviews* on *His Comfort and Joy*

"Jessica Bird's *A Man in a Million*
features a larger-than-life, irresistible hero and an equally
complex, intriguing heroine. Top-notch."
—*RT Book Reviews*

**Praise for #1 *New York Times* bestselling author
J. R. Ward**

"Terrific...explosive...exciting... Ward has outdone herself."
—*Publishers Weekly,* starred review on *Lover Enshrined*

"Ward wields a commanding voice perfect for the genre...
hold on tight for an intriguing, adrenaline-pumping ride."
—*Booklist* on *Lover Eternal*

"J. R. Ward has a great style of writing and she shines...
You will lose yourself in this world."
—*All About Romance* on *Dark Lover*

Also available from

J. R. Ward

written as Jessica Bird and HQN Books

THE REBEL

WRITING AS JESSICA BIRD

Recycling programs for this product may not exist in your area.

ISBN-13: 978-0-373-77641-2

THE PLAYER

Originally published as HIS COMFORT AND JOY

This edition published by arrangement with Harlequin Books S.A.

For questions and comments about the quality of this book please contact us at Customer_eCare@Harlequin.ca.

www.Harlequin.com

Printed in U.S.A.

Dear Reader,

As you know, I'm all about the alpha male—in whatever form he comes in! And although at the moment, I'm spending a lot of time with the vampire and fallen-angel variety of super-masculine hero, I started out with more "conventional" versions of these hard-headed, high-tempered, eminently sexy and lovable guys...including the one featured here. Originally published as *His Comfort and Joy,* this story about a powerful political consultant and the beautiful, innocent woman who captures his heart, features a particularly dangerous kind of alpha male: the player.

In the collective wisdom, players are those great-looking, sly-smiling types who always seem to know how to get a lady into...well, shall we say, a romantic frame of mind. They will sweep you off your feet, and show you the night of your life, but you shouldn't expect a relationship out of them because they're always too busy looking for the next best thing. Generally speaking, if you're approached by a player, you'll have a better outcome if the number you give him is your therapist's, instead of your own. 'Cuz, they've got issues....

In a lot of ways, Gray Bennett fits the player bill perfectly: suave, urbane and absolutely uninterested in being tied down to any one woman. He is unreachable, unattainable... and unreliable. He is also the man of Joy Moorehouse's dreams—literally. She's been fantasizing about him since she was a teenager, forever imagining what being with him would be like as she watches him from afar. And things might well have stayed on that level...if fate didn't find a way to bring them together.

Gray and Joy are not a match made in heaven—on the surface. They are at totally opposite ends of the dating spectrum, with him being so worldly and sophisticated, and her being sheltered and open-hearted. But Gray's bitterness and cynicism was learned at home, thanks to his mother, and he needs Joy's inherent goodness and lack of pretense to finally trust a woman enough to be vulnerable with her.

The single best thing about a player (and Gray)? When he finally gets tamed. Hands down, my favorite line in this book is from a scene where Gray and Joy go out on the town. She shows up in a borrowed dress that knocks his socks off and his reaction to not just what she's wearing, but also her attempt at big-city demeanor is pretty damned priceless:

> *Before he could say anything, a tuxedoed waiter appeared at their table. "Have you made your selections?"*
>
> *Um, yeah, Gray thought. I'll have the total body meltdown with a side of what-the-hell-was-I-thinking. She, evidently, will be having the sex-goddess pot pie.*

That still cracks me up! No matter how many women Gray has been with or how jaded he is, when the right one comes along, he falls like the best of them!

I really hope you enjoy this story of innocence and experience. In a lot of ways, it was a tribute to those Harlequin Presents and Silhouette Desire books I read way back when—the very ones that got me into the romance writing business. I love Gray and Joy for the way they remind me of the first Penny Jordans and Elizabeth Lowells that I read in the dark with a flashlight so many years ago, turning the pages so fast I sometimes tore them a little. I've had a love affair with love affairs all my life thanks to those books and those authors, and it's been such a privilege to get to write the kind of stories I once read with such abandon.

As always, wishing you happy reading,

J. R. Ward

With thanks to my first reader,
aka Mom

THE
PLAYER

CHAPTER ONE

THE BOAT'S ENGINE THROBBED as Grayson Bennett kept the Hacker at a low speed and close to the lakeshore. The antique, thirty-foot craft was his pride and joy, a relic of the Great Gatsby era of lake life. Made of mahogany and varnished to a shine so bright it could hurt your eyes, the *Bellitas* was indeed a thing of beauty. And she was wickedly fast. The long, thin design provided three discreet seating areas, marked by contoured banquettes in dark green leather. The massive engine, capable of shooting the boat through the water at speeds of sixty miles an hour, took up a good six feet of space in the middle.

He would miss her when he put her up on blocks for the winter, and the time for her yearly hibernation was coming fast. He could feel it in the air.

Even though it was the middle of the day, September was cool in the Adirondack Mountains of upstate New York. To take the edge off the chill, he was wearing a windbreaker and his only passenger, aside from a big, very happy golden retriever, had on a thick sweater.

Naturally, the dog had plenty of insulation.

Gray looked across the seat at the woman who stared at the cliffs they were passing. Cassandra Cutler's thick red hair was secured at her neck and her green eyes were hidden behind sunglasses. The frames covered up the dark circles of her exhaustion, too.

No doubt she saw little of the rocks and pine trees, he thought. Life had to be an inconsequential blur for someone who'd become a widow only six weeks ago.

"How're we doing?" he asked his old, dear friend.

She smiled slightly, a tense expression he knew she worked at. "I'm glad you pestered me to get out of the city."

"Good."

"I can't imagine I'm enjoyable company, though," Cassandra said.

"You're not here to perform."

Gray focused on the lake ahead as the silence was filled with the sound of the boat's deep-throated engine and the lapping of water against the wooden gunnels. Sunshine glinted off the mahogany, flashed over the tops of the gentle waves, brought out the vivid blue of the sky and the dense green of the mountains. The air was so clear and clean that when he breathed deep, the inside of his nose hummed.

It was a perfect fall day. And he was about to shoot the hell out of his quiet enjoyment.

When they'd left his estate's boathouse, he could have taken them in any direction. To the south, where they could have danced around a thicket of small islands. Across to the west to see some of the other big stretches of property.

But no, he'd chosen the north where sooner or later the old Moorehouse mansion would appear. White Caps was a big white birthday cake of a house, perched on a three-acre bluff. Once the family's lavish private home, it had been turned into a bed-and-breakfast by them when their money had run out.

But he wasn't going to look at the property.

When the bluff appeared in the distance, his eyes narrowed. The long rolling lawn, which drifted from White Caps' porches to the shore, was a dazzling green. Oaks and maples framed the house, already turning colors from the frosts that came at night.

He couldn't see anyone and he looked harder, even as he started to turn the boat around.

Cassandra didn't need to get anywhere near the Moorehouse place. Her husband's sailing partner, who'd survived the yachting accident, was recovering there with his family. Gray wasn't sure she knew that or whether she'd want to see Alex, but he wasn't inclined to take a chance at giving her another shock. She'd had enough bad surprises lately.

Cassandra's voice did not break his concentration. "My husband liked you, Gray."

"I liked Reese," he said, looking over his shoulder at the house, eyes searching.

"But he thought you were a dangerous man."

"Did he?"

"He said you knew where most of the bodies were buried in Washington, D.C. Because you'd put a lot of them in the ground."

He made a noise in the back of his throat and continued to stare as White Caps grew smaller.

"I've heard it from other people."

"Really."

"They say even the President is wary of you."

He glanced back at the house again. "Loose talk. Just loose talk."

"Considering the way you're looking at that mansion back there, I'm not so sure." Cassandra tilted her head to the side, regarding him with steady curiosity. "Who lives there? Or more to the point, what do you want that's in that house?"

When Gray remained silent, Cassandra's dry chuckle floated over on the breeze. "Well, whatever it is, I feel sorry for the poor thing. Because you look like you're on the hunt."

"HOLD STILL OR I'M GOING to stick you," Joy Moorehouse said to her sister.

"I am holding still."

"Then why is this hem a moving target?" She shifted back onto her heels and looked up at her work.

The wedding gown hung from her sister Frankie's shoulders in a graceful fall of white satin. Joy had been careful with the design. Too many frills and excess fabric wouldn't pass muster. Frankie thought blue jeans were formal as long as you wore them with your hair up.

"Do I look like I'm in someone else's dress?" Frankie asked.

"You look beautiful."

Frankie laughed without bitterness. "That's your department, not mine. I'm the plain, practical sister, remember?"

"Ah, but you're the one getting married."

"And ain't it a miracle?"

Joy smiled. "I'm so happy for you."

Everyone was. The whole town of Saranac Lake was thrilled and they were all coming to festivities that were taking place in about six weeks.

Frankie lifted the skirting up gingerly, as if she might hurt it. "I have to admit, this thing feels good."

"It'll fit even better when I finish the alterations. You can take it off now."

"We're done?"

Joy nodded and got up from the floor. "I've basted all around the bottom. I'll stitch it up this evening and we'll do another fitting tomorrow."

"But I thought you were going to help out tonight. We're catering Mr. Bennett's birthday party, remember?"

Joy almost laughed. She'd have better luck losing track of her own head than forgetting where she was supposed to be in another couple of hours. And who she would see.

"Remember?" Frankie prompted. "We're going to need you."

Joy made busywork putting her sewing kit back together. She had a feeling her excitement was showing on her face and she didn't want her sister to see it. "I know."

"The party could go late."

"It doesn't matter." Because it wasn't as if she'd be able to sleep when they got back home.

"I don't want you slaving over this dress."

"And you're getting married in a month and a half, so I have to get the thing done. Well, unless you fancy yourself heading down the aisle in your underwear, a sight I'm pretty sure Nate would prefer to keep for his eyes only. Besides, you know I love doing this, especially for you." She turned around. Her sister was staring out the window, absently stroking the gown. "Frankie? What's wrong?"

"Last night, I asked Alex to walk me to the altar."

"What did he say?" Joy whispered, even though she knew getting their brother to the ceremony at all was going to be tough.

"He won't do it. I don't think he wants the attention to be on him." Frankie shook her head. "I can't force him to be by my side. But I really wish…hell, I wish Dad were going to be with me. Mom, as well. I wish they were both still here."

Joy took her sister's hand. "Me, too."

Frankie looked down at herself, her brown hair falling forward. She gave a short, awkward laugh that Joy knew meant she was changing the subject. "I can't believe this."

"What?"

"I don't want to take this thing off. It's so gorgeous."

Joy smiled sadly, thinking that with each stitch she put into the gown, she was trying to make up for everything her sister had done for her. God, all those sacrifices Frankie had made to become a parent too soon. The work on the dress seemed like a pitiful exchange.

"Here, let me undo the buttons in the back for you."

When Frankie stepped out of the pool of satin, Joy swept the dress into her arms and carried it over to her worktable. Her bedroom was small, so between her sewing machine, her mannequin and the bolts of fabric against the wall, space was at a premium. Thank God she only had a twin bed.

Over the years she'd patched and repaired countless ball gowns for their grandmother at her little makeshift sewing station. Emma Moorehouse, better known as Grand-Em, suffered from dementia so she was prone to irrational obsessions. And given that she'd once been a wealthy young lady of fine breeding and reputation, she felt uncomfortable if she didn't look her best for the parties she was certain were just about to start every moment of the day.

Except there were no parties. There hadn't been for decades.

With the declining fortunes of the Moorehouse family, there was no money to replace either the lifestyle or the luxury their grandmother had once known. But Joy was able to keep the Golden Era illusion alive by maintaining the forty- and fifty-year-old ball gowns. In doing so, she helped Grand-Em to find a measure of calm.

And discovered a passion for clothing design in herself.

"We've got three rooms filled this weekend," Frankie said as she pulled on khakis. "Which means the leaf peepers are showing up on schedule."

The White Caps mansion had been built by their ancestors at the turn of the nineteenth century and back then, it had been one of many Moorehouse real estate holdings. Now the ten-bedroom house was all that was left of a once mighty fortune.

In the eighties, their mother and father had turned the place into a bed-and-breakfast. Following their deaths a decade ago, Frankie had struggled to keep the business going, and it appeared that they'd finally turned a corner. The B&B was on the upswing, thanks in large part to Frankie's fiancé, Nate Walker. Nate's fine French cooking had made White Caps a destination and his timely investment in the business had pulled them out of a debt spiral.

"So, about tonight." Frankie shoved her feet into a pair of beat-up sneakers. "Spike's going to mind the store here with George on backup. Nate, Tom and I are going to head over to the Bennett kitchen in another hour or so. Can you get there about five?"

"No problem."

"Thank God, Alex is willing to watch Grand-Em. Have you told him what to expect?"

Joy nodded. "I think he'll be okay and Spike's here if she gets really agitated. Fortunately she's been quieter now during evenings."

Stewarding Grand-Em through her delusions was usually Joy's job, but they needed all the hands they could get for the party.

"I'm so glad Gray gave us this chance," Frankie said, drawing her hair back. "He's a good man. For a politician."

He's not a politician, Joy wanted to say. He's a political consultant who specializes in elections.

But the correction might get her sister's attention and Joy was careful about keeping her obsession with Gray to herself. Sharing pipe dreams was almost as futile as having them in the first place.

"You're awful quiet, Joy. Are you sure you want to come tonight?"

"I'm just distracted." By the fact that she was going to get to watch Gray for three, maybe four, hours. And that maybe she'd get a chance to talk with him.

Although the exposure probably wasn't a good thing. After so many years of pining for the man, lately she'd been trying to let the unrequited fascination go. She was going to be twenty-seven soon, for heaven's sake. Living in the fantasy was getting old. And so was she.

"You don't have to come, Joy. I could have one of the waitresses sub."

"I want to," she said firmly.

Sort of.

Because he was going to look so good tonight. Grayson Bennett always looked good.

"You work too hard," Frankie said.

"So do you."

Frankie shook her head and then stared long and hard across the room. She'd worn glasses until recently, and without the lenses, her eyes seemed bluer than ever.

"You know," she said casually, "I was talking to Tom yesterday. He was asking a lot of questions about you. He's a really nice guy."

Tom Reynolds was the new line cook who'd been hired to help Nate and his partner, Spike, in the kitchen. And he was a nice guy. With a nice guy's sweet smile. And a nice guy's gentle eyes. And a nice guy's polite manner.

Except Joy liked what Gray had. The power. The charisma. The promise of breathtaking, hot sex.

Which probably would have shocked her sister.

If Frankie was the practical one, Joy was supposed to be the prim, protected youngest. Except she was getting bored with being good, especially whenever Gray Bennett came to mind.

Which, in spite of her resolve, was about as often as the grandfather clock downstairs spoke up.

Basically, every fifteen minutes.

"Maybe you and Tom should go out sometime," Frankie said.

Joy shrugged. "Maybe."

As her sister left the room, Joy sat on the bed. She knew her fixation on Gray was unhealthy. Getting tangled up in fantasies about some man she saw maybe five or six times a year was ridiculous. And it wasn't as if he encouraged her. Whenever Gray came up to the lake in the summer and she ran into him in town, he was always friendly. He even remembered her name. But that was as far as it ever got.

Well, except in her dreams. Then it went a whole lot further.

In real life, however, the attraction was totally one-sided. She was pretty certain about how Gray perceived her and it was just what she thought of Tom, the line cook. Nice. Sweet. Young.

Completely unremarkable.

And the truly pathetic thing was, even though she knew all that, even though she wanted to forget about Grayson Bennett, she still couldn't wait to see him tonight.

GRAY WORKED HIS FATHER'S TIE into a Windsor knot. Ever since the stroke five months ago, Walter Bennett's left side wasn't working right. The physical rehab helped, and with time's passing his brain had recovered some, but his fine motor skills were still compromised.

"You ready for tonight, Papa?"

"Yes. I. Am." The words were slow and slightly garbled.

"Well, you look sharp as hell." Gray measured his efforts. A little tug to the right and the tie was perfect.

Walter tapped his chest with a gnarled hand, pushing aside the strip of bright red silk. "Happy. Very. Happy."

"Me, too." Gray smoothed the tie back into place.

"Are. You?"

Gray walked over to the bureau and picked up his father's gold cuff links. They were heavy in his hand, marked with the Bennett family crest. He had a pair just like them, given to him when he'd turned eighteen and headed off to Harvard.

His father stamped his foot, a habit he'd developed when he had to get someone's attention. "Are. You?"

"Sure."

"Don't. Lie." Walter was stooped with age, far shorter than he'd been when he'd had his youth, but he was still a big man. And although he wasn't fierce by nature, not like his only son, when he wanted to be, he could be very direct. The trait was no doubt one of the reasons he'd been such a successful federal judge in D.C.

Gray smiled to reassure his father. "I'm looking forward to getting back to Washington."

Which was lie number two.

Walter huffed as his cuff links were put on and Gray had the feeling he was being given a stiff lecture in his father's head.

"You. Should. Talk. More."

"About what?"

"You."

"There are much better subjects. Besides, you know the Dr. Phil stuff's never been my thing." Gray stepped back. "Okay, Papa. You're done. I need to shower and change."

"Change," his father said. "Change. Is. Good."

Gray nodded, but cut off the conversation by heading for his own room. On his way down the hall, he paused in front of Cassandra's guest room.

And sometimes change wasn't so good.

After he'd learned about Cassandra's husband's death, Gray had made a point of going to New York

City to see her in person. He'd worried that with Reese gone, she'd be all alone in the midst of the Manhattan social tilt-a-whirl. Fortunately, their mutual friend, Allison Adams, and her husband, the senator, had taken to watching over the new widow like a hawk. But it was still a difficult time.

If Gray and Allison hadn't ridden her so hard, Cass never would have agreed to come up for the weekend. She'd have continued to nurse her broken heart in that big penthouse on Park Avenue all by herself.

Gray kept walking. Cassandra and Allison were two unusual women for the circles he ran in. They loved their husbands and were faithful to them.

Which was why Reese's death struck him as unfair.

Most of the ladies Gray knew, and he used the term *lady* loosely, thought fidelity was something you had for a clothing or shoe designer. The fact that some sap slid a diamond on their finger and they'd thrown on a white dress made little impression on their libidos.

But maybe he was just bitter.

Yeah, only a little, he thought.

Gray shut the door to his room and took off his polo shirt. He'd had a lot of women come on to him over the years and a good number had been married. But he couldn't blame his distrust of the fairer sex solely on his contemporaries.

No, he'd learned his first lessons at home.

From mommy dearest.

Belinda Bennett was a blue-blooded, well-moneyed beauty. Real top-drawer stuff if you looked at her *Mayflower* roots and all that patrician bone structure. Unfortunately, she was first and foremost a harlot.

A rebellious, misbehaving, spoiled brat who seemed determined to make her mark on her back.

As if getting screwed by men who didn't give a damn about her was a badge of independence.

God, the things she'd done to his father. The humiliation. The degradation. And all of it caused by what she'd done with his friends at the club. His tax attorney. His own cousin. As well as the gardener, her tennis instructor, the choir master.

Hell, even Gray's camp counselor and his prep school English professor hadn't been off-limits. And she'd also managed to find her way into the pants of two of his buddies from college. Former buddies, that was.

Gray turned the shower on, kicked off his shorts and stepped under the water.

His father was a good man. Weak when it came to love, but a good man. Unfortunately, this combination meant he'd stayed in the marriage even though he'd known what was happening. Even though his heart had gotten broken over and over.

Which was precisely what happened when your principles outweighed your common sense. You got spanked.

Courtesy of the spectacle, Gray had decided long ago never to let a woman get into his head, much less the center of his chest. He'd been called a misogynist by quite a number of them, and though that was hardly something he was proud of, he'd never denied the charge.

Gray couldn't imagine trying out what his father had attempted and failed at. He couldn't fathom the idea of finding a woman he could really trust and marrying her.

Ah, hell. Maybe he was just a coward.

Gray snorted as he stepped out of the shower and toweled off.

Yeah, and if he was such a pansy, why were so many members of the Senate and the House of Representatives scared of him? And the President of the United States might not be wary, but he sure as hell took Gray's calls, no matter where the man was, no matter who he was with.

No, it wasn't cowardice that had him pulling the I-am-an-island routine. It was a complete lack of myopia. He saw clearly the truth other men didn't. If you gave anyone the power to hurt you, soon enough, they were going to use it.

Gray walked into his closet, picked out a navy-blue suit and a button-down shirt, and tossed them onto the bed. He pulled on the pants and was zipping them up when he caught a flash of movement outside.

His hands stilled and he leaned toward the window.

He'd know that strawberry-blond hair anywhere.

Joy Moorehouse was coming down his driveway on a bicycle, her long mane of curls streaming out behind her like a flag. She pulled up to the side of the house, looked around and seemed to realize she'd overshot the service entrance. Slipping off the bike, she walked it around to the back, away from view.

Gray's body slammed into overdrive, his blood pumping, his muscles twitching as if he were about to run after her.

He cursed and planted his hands on his hips.

This was not happening, he thought. He was not feeling any of this.

Yeah, whatever.

And then, as if his libido were taking a potshot at

him, he was subjected to a quick replay of the day he'd caught her in nothing more than a bikini.

God, that had been a couple of weeks ago, but he could picture it as clear as if it had happened this morning.

To think he'd once considered his accurate recall a gift.

After years of seeing Joy around town during the summers, and finding her pretty but otherwise unassuming, something had changed this season. And that was before he'd gone to White Caps and come upon her just as she was about to take a swim.

Lovely before, she'd become instantly a thing of legend. Those subtle curves, all that smooth skin, those eyes so startled and wide when she'd seen him.

Frankly, he was appalled with himself. She was so young. Well, maybe not that young, but there was something so pure about her. So guileless. So honest. She was fresh in a way that made him feel as though he should wash his hands before he dared touch her.

Hell, with all her innocence, she made him feel dirty and ancient. Dirty for the things he'd done. Old because he had nothing but cynicism and hard ambition to offer anybody.

Gray cursed again and yanked on his shirt. The buttons refused to behave well under his fingers and it took him twice as long as it usually did to get the thing done up. And forget about the cuff links. He actually dropped one.

As he crammed the shirttails into the waistband of his pants, the fact that he was suddenly in a rush to get dressed and go downstairs didn't escape him.

But it sure as hell didn't improve his mood.

CHAPTER TWO

JOY PROPPED HER BIKE against the house and looked around. She'd grown up in a big place, but Gray's mansion was huge. The three-story structure was the size of a college dorm and looked like a castle. It was also in perfect shape, the great stone walls pale and clean in the late sun, the trim painted bright white, the shutters gleaming black.

"Yea, you're here!" Frankie's voice came out an open screen door. "How'd you like to help make cream puffs?"

Joy swept her hair up and pinned it out of the way with a barrette as she came into the industrial-quality kitchen. "I'm your girl. Just show me—"

The force of the blow sent her reeling into the wall and nearly kicked her feet out from under her. Something hit her in a wet splatter and then there was a loud clang as a pan bounced on the floor. The kitchen went dead quiet.

Tom Reynolds's face was the color of oatmeal. Although it wasn't as if he'd had a deep tan to begin with.

"Oh, God. Are you okay?" He reached out. "I didn't see you. I'm so sorry. I'm really, really..."

Joy glanced down at herself. Her white shirt and black pants were covered with tortellini and pesto. She looked as though she'd been stabbed and was bleeding brilliant green.

Right out of a Roger Corman flick, she thought with a grin.

"I'm fine." She was more worried about Tom. He didn't look so steady. "Trust me, I'll recover."

The poor guy was on the verge of another round of apologies, but Frankie's fiancé cut him off with a hand to the back of the neck.

"Whoa, tiger. What was I telling you about slowing down?" Nate was a big, handsome man dressed in jeans and a black T-shirt. He looked about as cheflike as your average Harley motorcycle owner, but he was heaven on wheels behind a stove. "You all right, angel?"

She smiled at her soon-to-be brother-in-law. "Fine and dandy. Just keep me away from the vampires. I could give a garlic wreath a run for the money."

Frankie came over, shaking her head. "We're going to have to get you out of those clothes. I think I saw some waitressing uniforms in the back room. Let me see what I can find."

Nate got down on his hands and knees and started cleaning up the mess. "We're going to have to get creative. There isn't enough time to remake this batch so we'll have to whip up something else."

Tom sank to the floor, putting his head between his knees for a moment. His blond hair was messed up as if even his follicles were upset.

"I really need this job," he said softly.

Nate froze. "Who said you were getting canned? Good God, you should know half the things I've dropped over the years."

Joy put her hand on Tom's shoulder. "It was just

an accident. I should have been looking where I was going, too."

The cook blushed as he began scooping up tortellini with his hands. "That's a nice thing for you to say, Joy."

A second later Frankie came back with a black-and-white uniform in her arms and an impish, sixty-year-old woman at her side.

"Oh, look at the poor girl," the woman said, grabbing the clean clothes. "Come on, now, I'll show you to a shower."

As Joy's hand was taken in a firm, warm grip, she let herself get swept along.

"I'm Libby, Old Mr. Bennett's housekeeper." They went up a set of back stairs. "I suppose I'm his butler and his secretary when he's here, too. I'm also Ernest's mom."

"Ernest?"

"He's not allowed in the kitchen when we're cooking. Although he'd be handy at cleaning up that pasta."

At the top of the stairs, they turned right and went down a hall. On the walls there were black-and-white photographs of sporting events hung from floor to ceiling. Joy slowed. There were staid ones from the 1920s, with men dressed formally for cricket and a woman with her hair cut into a bob twirling on old-fashioned ice skates. A football team picture from the forties had all the players wearing leather helmets and big *H*s on their chests. There was a shot of a track-and-field event from the seventies, with a man wearing first-generation Nikes vaulting over a pole. Another picture was taken at a swim meet with a girl diving fiercely into the water.

"Ah, yes, the Bennetts over the generations," Libby said fondly. "They're an athletic lot, aren't they? I put up the pictures because I couldn't stand to have them lying around, collecting dust in boxes. And wouldn't you know? Gray and his father both make a point to take first-time visitors up here to witness the glory."

Joy stepped forward only to pause again. In a simple black frame, she saw four men standing in front of a crew boat, their arms linked. Gray was on the end, grinning.

"Oh, I like that one, too," Libby said. "Young Mr. Bennett looks so happy in it."

The woman went down further and opened a door. A golden retriever bounded out into the hall, eighty or so pounds of glee in a pale fur suit. After a quick lick of Libby's hands, he headed straight for Joy.

Libby did her best to quell the adoration, but Joy didn't care. She was perfectly happy to be climbed on.

"Ernest likes you," his mom muttered while trying to grab his collar.

With a lunge into the air, the dog leaped up, his front paws nearly shoulder height. Joy laughed and gave his sides a sturdy round of patting.

"I'm not sure I should take it personally," she said. "I smell like Italian food, so what's not to love?"

After Ernest found a tortellini in the folds of her shirt, she went into the room. It was beautifully decorated with flowered wallpaper and lots of drapes. A four-poster bed with handmade quilts folded at the foot took up most of the space. The rest was occupied by antiques.

"This is lovely," Joy said, thinking of the staff quarters back at White Caps. Those rooms were like prison cells in comparison.

"The Bennetts take very good care of me. And Ernest. Young Mr. Bennett's practically adopted him."

"He likes dogs?"

Man, if Gray Bennett was a canine lover, that would pretty much seal the deal on him being a total dreamboat.

"Don't know about all dogs, but he loves Ernest. They go on walks together and boat rides and—" Libby shook her head. "I'm rambling. The shower's through there. You'll find fresh towels on the rack and there's a hair dryer under the sink. I'd have taken you to another room, but the other staff quarters are shut down for the winter and the guest rooms are all filled. Do you mind if Ernest stays?"

Joy looked at the dog who returned her gaze with inquiry.

"Of course not." She smiled and fluffed his soft ear.

As his owner left, Ernest planted his butt on the floor and leaned into Joy's leg.

"So, Gray's your buddy," she said to the dog when the door closed. "Got any secrets you'd like to share?"

GRAY PUSHED OPEN the butler's door and strode into the kitchen.

"Hey, big guy," Nate called from the counter. "You're lookin' fine tonight."

They shook hands with a meaty clap. White Caps' new chef had turned out to be someone Gray knew well. He and Nate had gone to college together, though they'd lost touch thereafter. It had been a real kick in the pants, in a good way, to find out who'd transformed the Moorehouses' kitchen into paradise.

But then life could be like that. Six degrees to the

right or left and you were staring your past in the face again.

"Everything smells terrific," Gray said while scanning the room. He waved at Frankie, who was lining up dozens and dozens of dough balls on stainless-steel trays. There was another guy bent over the stove, someone he didn't recognize.

Where was she? he wondered. Or was he totally losing it and had only imagined seeing Joy on his lawn?

"You need anything?" he asked, stalling.

"Nah, we're all good." Nate went back to mincing up parsley with a vicious-looking knife. "Everything's under control."

There was a pause and Gray became aware that everyone was working except for him.

Ah, hell. He couldn't very well stand here like a wallflower.

The butler's door swung open behind him.

"There you are," Cassandra said. "There's someone on the phone for you. Libby's been running around the house looking everywhere."

As the heads in the room turned in her direction, Cassandra smiled. "Sorry to interrupt."

Gray measured her expression as she looked at Frankie. There was no sign of recognition on her face. Or Frankie's, either. Good Lord, the two women didn't know each other.

He cleared his throat. "Cassandra, this is Frankie Moorehouse. Alex's sister. Frankie, Cassandra Cutler. Reese's…widow."

Cassandra paled, her hand coming to her throat. Frankie had a similar reaction, straightening slowly in shock.

Damn it, he should have warned them both, he thought, feeling like a heel. He'd just assumed that they knew who the other was.

Frankie came forward, wiping the flour from her hands with a side towel. "I'm so sorry about Reese."

Cassandra reached out. "Your brother. Is he all right? I'd heard when the coast guard found him he was injured."

Frankie nodded. "He's recovering. It's going to be a long haul, though."

"When he didn't come to the funeral, and he didn't call, I worried…" Cassandra's voice broke. "I can only imagine what he's going through. He and Reese were closer than sailing partners. They were like brothers. Where is he?"

"Here. At home."

"I must see him."

Frankie took a deep breath. "You're welcome to, but you should be prepared. He's, ah, not really open to conversation. Although maybe you can reach him. We sure haven't been able to."

Gray noticed that Cassandra's body was shaking and he slipped his arm around her waist. She leaned into him.

"I'd certainly like to try," she said. "I want to know what happened on that boat."

AS JOY LEFT LIBBY'S QUARTERS, she corralled Ernest with her leg, somehow keeping him inside the room. She felt like a jailer and it was hard not giving in to the dog's pleading eyes. Staring up at her, he was on the verge of speech, desperate for clemency.

Except there was no way she was going to buy the

whole saint's-preserve-me, I'm-just-a-meek-fellow routine. And having already experienced one catastrophe this evening, she didn't want to chance what would happen if the retriever got loose in a kitchen with Tom Reynolds. The two could probably level the whole house.

As she went down the stairs, she wondered when she'd run into Gray. She figured it probably wouldn't be until the party started, so she had at least another forty-five minutes to prepare herself. Coming around the corner into the kitchen, she smoothed the uniform, thinking at least the thing fit her. The skirt was a little short, but other than that it looked decent—

She skidded to a halt.

Gray Bennett was standing by the stove, looking better than any man had a right to. His dark hair was brushed back from his arrogant face. His broad shoulders and chest filled up a beautifully tailored navy-blue jacket. And the faint pink of his button-down shirt brought out his tan and his pale blue eyes.

The only thing that ruined the picture was the fact that he had his arm around a woman. And he was looking down at her face as if he cared deeply for her.

Joy's stomach heaved.

Oh, God.

She actually considered running back upstairs, but forced herself to stay put. After all, she was being utterly ridiculous. A man like him wouldn't live the life of a monk. And she'd read plenty of stories in the papers about who he was out with in D.C. So the fact that he had a woman really shouldn't be a surprise.

Except it was. Whenever he'd come to Saranac Lake,

he'd always been alone. She'd never actually seen him with someone firsthand.

And of course, the woman was a beauty. Thick red hair, pale, translucent skin, green eyes that were looking curiously distraught. And the cream dress she was wearing? It was so perfectly simple, the fabric so gorgeous, the fit so precise, it had to be haute couture.

They were perfect together.

Joy looked back at Gray and was startled. His eyes had narrowed into beams and they were trained on her. Which wouldn't have bothered her ordinarily except he did not seem happy. The simmering darkness in his face was dismaying. In the past, he'd always been friendly to her. Why was he suddenly looking at her as if she wasn't welcome in his house?

"Tom, would you like some help with the filet?" she asked, quickly going over to where the cook was cutting up beef.

"That would be great," Tom said, making room for her at the counter. "Here's a knife."

As she went to work, she was shaken and trying not to show it. Seeing Gray looking so good was hard. Catching him with his hand on some redhead's hip was worse. But getting stared down by the man was nearly unbearable.

When she looked over her shoulder a while later, Gray had left and taken the Julianne Moore look-alike with him.

But what Joy saw was a real zinger anyway.

Nate was standing behind Frankie and had pulled her back against his body. He was whispering something in her ear as she bent over the cream puffs. His face was tight with hunger and Frankie had a half smile on her face as if she liked what he was saying to her. Joy looked away quickly.

"They sure are happy," Tom said.

Of course, they were. Because what they had was real, not some childish, one-sided fantasy.

Joy thought back to the nights she'd stayed up imagining different ways she'd run into Gray. There were so many. Maybe they'd meet in town, just passing by on the sidewalk. He'd stop and tell her it was hot out and ask her if she wanted something cool to drink. Or maybe she was on an island out on the lake and he'd go by in one of his boats. He'd catch sight of her and pull into the dock and they'd lie in the sun. The scenarios were like little plays she directed and the outcome always ended with them kissing.

Daydreams, she thought. Fantasies. With all of it, down to the clothes he wore and the way he looked at her, existing only in her mind.

As she thought about the way Nate stared at Frankie, she couldn't bear her pathetic hallucinations.

"Tom, would you like to go out to dinner with me?" she blurted.

The cook's mouth actually fell open as he stopped slicing and glanced up. He looked as though someone had just offered him a free Mercedes-Benz. "Well, yeah."

"Tomorrow night. Pick me up at seven?"

"Sure. I mean, I'd love to."

Joy nodded and went back to work. "Good."

CHAPTER THREE

BY THE END OF THE EVENING, as the guests were either heading home to their own houses or retiring to the bedrooms upstairs, Gray categorically considered the party a success. His father had a glow on his face that had been missing for months. The food had been sublime. People had had a great time.

But he was just as happy to have it over. He'd wanted to escape for the last hour although it wasn't because he'd been overwhelmed by the guests. Fifty people was a good-size party, but nothing like the four- or five-hundred-head social endurance tests he did regularly in D.C.

No, the problem was Joy.

He'd given himself whiplash searching the crowd for her. Every time he saw a flash of black and white, his head flipped around, but rarely had it been the woman he'd wanted to see. Over the course of the evening, he'd only caught a couple glimpses of her passing hors d'oeuvres or picking up empty glasses. She seemed to stay far away from him, as if on purpose.

Hell, that uniform was a knockout on her, so he should probably be grateful.

Gray went into his study and tore off his jacket, tossing the thing onto the back of a chesterfield sofa.

He removed his cuff links, put them in his pocket and rolled up his sleeves.

He was fixing himself a bourbon when the U.S. Senate Majority Leader walked into the room.

Gray nodded over his shoulder. "Hey, Becks. You want to join me?"

"Just add plenty of rocks," John Beckin said with his trademark glossy smile. The expression lightened his air of masculine distinction. With his silver hair combed back from a strong face and horn-rimmed glasses perched on his straight nose, the man's aura was one of intelligence and discretion, and it wasn't all image. He'd clerked for Gray's father straight out of law school in the seventies and had been smart as a whip even then. The two were still close.

Gray handed over a squat crystal glass with two inches of liquor and three cubes of ice in it.

"Thanks. Listen, I wanted to catch you alone," John said, shutting the door. "How's Walter really doing?"

As a career politician, and a very successful one, Becks knew how to project sympathy and understanding. In this case, Gray thought the emotions were probably real.

"Better every day." He poured a glass for himself, neat. "But this is the first time you've seen him in person, right?"

"I have to tell you, it was a shock. His e-mails sounded so positive, but it's obviously hard for him to get around. And his speech…" John shook his head. "But hell, Gray, I don't mean to be negative. He looked happy tonight. Especially when you were toasting him. That man couldn't be more proud of you."

"Thanks."

"Has Belinda been by?"

Gray tossed back the bourbon, draining the glass in two swallows. The liquor burned his gut. Or maybe that was just his anger at his mother. "No, she hasn't."

And she knew better than to try if he was around.

John put a hand in his pocket and went over to a window. "You know, since my Mary died, I've been reminiscing a lot more than I used to. These last two years have been hard for me, and I was thinking, as I saw you with your father, that he'd be so alone without you. Children are a blessing. I'm sorry that Mary and I never had any."

Gray kept his mouth shut. As children were not in his future, he didn't feel qualified to comment on them.

There was a silence and then John seemed to shake himself out of the mood he'd sunk into. When he turned, his face was intense.

"So, I must tell you something I've heard."

Gray cocked an eyebrow. "You know how I like your news flashes."

"Well, this one I'm not happy about. You recall those stories in the paper about certain internal disputes in the Senate? Written by the acerbic and nosy Ms. Anna Shaw?"

"I've read them. Sounds like you boys have a leak."

"We do. And I know who it is." John finished his drink, the ice tinkling musically against the crystal. "I'm afraid one of my fellow senators is having an affair with Shaw."

Gray poured himself another shot of bourbon. "And you know this because?"

"The lovely Anna was seen coming out of the man's

hotel room. During the Democratic National Convention."

"How does that equate with an affair? Maybe he was giving her an interview."

"It was 4:00 a.m. She was wearing a raincoat with nothing under it. And it wasn't the first time."

"Well, that was stupid. On both their parts." He brought his drink up to his lips.

"It was Senator Adams."

Gray froze, looking over the rim of his glass. "Excuse me?"

"Roger Adams."

As in *Allison's* husband? "You sure?"

"You think I'd make up something like this?"

"Son of a bitch." Gray put the bourbon down. Allison and Roger Adams were hardly front-runners for marital problems. Not by a long shot.

"Now, it's none of my business who sleeps with who on the Hill." John started to move around the room, looking at the leather-bound books on the shelves. "God knows, you can't swing a dead cat without hitting an adulterer in that town. But I resent the hell out of a man who cheats on his wife while holding himself out to be a feminist. Adams is trying to bring another Equal Rights Amendment to the floor, for God's sakes. He's made a point to support women's causes."

Goddamn, Gray thought. Roger Adams.

Never would have seen that one coming. And Allison probably wouldn't have, either.

John rattled his ice. "I have to tell you, the fact that the idiot picks a reporter and spills our secrets to her while he's taking her to bed really ticks me off."

The senator paused and looked across the room.

There was calculation in his face and Gray's eyes narrowed.

"I have the feeling you're not just passing along gossip," Gray drawled. "Don't beat around the bush, Becks. What do you want from me?"

The Majority Leader had the grace to flush. "My fellow senators come to you for advice. They seek you out not just because you're smart, but because you've gotten the most powerful of them elected. I want you to warn the others. Adams isn't to be trusted. Not anymore. I'd do it myself, but they'd look through party lines and figure I was just trying to screw the guy."

Gray smiled sardonically. "And you're not? Not even considering he blocked your attempt to loosen up the campaign finance reform bill in the last session?"

"See, this is my point exactly. That's what everyone will think when really I'm just trying to keep my Senate protected."

His Senate. Not the American people's.

Gray felt a wave of exhaustion come over him, like someone had thrown a wet wool blanket over his head. He was getting tired of Capitol Hill and its intrigues, he really was.

"Look, Gray, I'll give you the names of my sources. Check out the stories yourself. And then help me put an end to these salacious articles. That reporter is making a mockery out of our political process and that gum-flapping Democrat is helping her do it."

The door to the study burst open.

Joy pulled up short, an empty tray hanging from her hand. "Oh, I'm sorry. I was looking for the library."

Becks smiled paternally, the hard tone in his voice

disappearing completely. "Not to worry, my dear. An interruption from the likes of you is no hardship."

She looked flustered. "I'll just come back for the empty glasses in here later—"

"Not at all. I'm leaving." The senator put down his drink and smiled at Gray. "We'll talk soon and thank you again for including me tonight. It meant a lot just to see Walter again. He did so much for me when I was getting started."

As Becks left, Joy stared at his face as if trying to place the man. Then she shook her head. "I'll sweep this room later."

She turned away. And Gray couldn't let her go.

"Joy. Wait."

She hesitated, back straight as a wall. When he went over to her, she did not look at him.

Good Lord, she was so lovely.

The light from overhead fell down on the delicate planes of her face and brought out the golds and pale reds of her hair. Her long, slender neck was set off by the short white-lace collar of the uniform, her collarbones just barely exposed by the cut of the blouse. Even at the end of a long night, she smelled like lavender.

Gray burned.

"Let me help you," he said roughly.

Let me kiss you, he thought. Just once.

Impatience flickered over her features, tightening the lips he stared at. "That's not necessary. Really."

As if she'd have preferred to be aided by a gorilla.

"I want to."

He polished off the bourbon he'd put down, reached for the senator's glass, which was close by, and cocked his eyebrow. She brought up the tray and he put the crystal on it.

"I don't need your help."

"Yes, you've already pointed that out," he murmured, taking the tray from her.

JOY SWALLOWED A GROAN. She didn't want to get anywhere near Gray. Not now. Not when she was trying so hard to put her crush to bed.

She winced. Bad choice of words.

"Shall we?" he said in that low rumble of his.

She glanced up and was unable to look further than the top button of his shirt.

The width of his shoulders was enough to block her view of the room entirely and he towered over her, making her feel small. She looked down a little, hoping he'd feel shorter that way. Instead she just noticed that he'd taken off his jacket and rolled up his sleeves. His forearms were muscular with veins that ran down into his long, sure hands.

"Don't you have something else to do?" she demanded.

Couldn't he go save the world or something and let her finish her job in peace?

"Nope."

Joy gritted her teeth and walked across the hall into a parlor. Going through the beautifully appointed room, she picked up empties and put them on the tray he held. As they moved around, she could feel him looming behind her and she could have sworn his eyes were on her body.

Stop it, she told herself. She knew damn well that

was just her fantasies talking. He was only helping her out, probably thought he was being chivalrous.

When they were finished there, they went into the library she'd been looking for in the first place. With only the sound of his loafers and her flats on the marble floor, the silence started to get to her.

She couldn't stand it anymore.

"So who was that man you were talking to? I feel like I've seen him before."

"Just a politician."

Somehow she doubted that. "I think I've seen him on TV."

"You might have."

"Actually, I think I've seen a lot of the people here tonight on CNN."

She walked past an antique table and realized she'd missed a glass. Stopping abruptly, she bent over to grab it.

And Gray walked right into her body.

His hips connected with her backside, brushing against her intimately. The fit was shocking.

But what really got her attention was the fact that she felt something hard.

He hissed and stepped back. "Sorry, I didn't see you."

She grabbed the glass with two hands, afraid she was going to drop it. As she carefully put it on the tray, she looked up.

Gray's eyes drilled into hers, twin beams of pale blue shooting through the tense air between them.

She forgot how to breathe.

After years of fantasizing about Grayson Bennett,

the legend, she was actually being stared at with wild lust by Grayson Bennett, the man.

A woman's voice broke the moment, splitting through it like an ax. "I finally found you."

Joy looked around Gray's shoulder.

The redhead walked into the room, as comfortable and relaxed as if she owned the place.

"I'm heading up for bed," she said. And then had the gall to smile at Joy.

Joy grabbed the tray and made a beeline for the door, feeling like a fool. As she rushed for the kitchen, body shaking like a paint mixer, she cursed herself.

When heavy footsteps came after her, she walked faster.

"Joy." Gray's voice was all command. "Joy!"

She stopped. And truly hated him at that moment.

God, was he going to apologize? Or worse, suggest they meet up after he'd finished with his girlfriend? Damn it, she'd known he was out of her league, but had assumed it was because he was rich and handsome and powerful. Instead he was all that and a total player.

"Joy, I'd like you to meet Cassandra."

Joy closed her eyes and prayed for composure.

Oh, this was great. He wanted to *introduce* them.

She squared her shoulders before turning around.

The redhead was at Gray's side, looking both sad and a little amused as she smiled in greeting.

"I'm Reese's wife," the woman murmured softly.

Joy felt the blood drain out of her head. "Oh, I didn't know…."

"Of course you didn't," Cassandra said graciously. "I think you came downstairs just after the introductions were made."

While Joy stuttered out her condolences, Gray put his hand on the redhead's shoulder. It was the perfect reminder of the kind of relationship the two had, and as soon as Joy could, she retreated into the kitchen. She felt awful for Cassandra's loss, and the woman did look pained. But it wasn't hard to believe that seeking solace in Gray's arms would be a relief from her sorrow.

Joy put the glasses down next to the industrial dishwasher that had almost finished a load. The kitchen was spotless. Nate, Frankie and Tom were an efficient team and had gotten the cleanup done in record time.

"We're ready to head out," Frankie said to her. "The Honda and Tom's truck are all loaded up."

"I'll just wait to put in these last few glasses and then I'll head home."

"You want me to come back and get you?" Nate asked, untying the long white apron that covered his jeans.

"I'll be fine. It's not like there's a lot of traffic on the Lake Road this time of year." And she could really use the air to clear her head.

Frankie gave her back the clothes that had suffered the tortellini onslaught. They were folded in a neat pile. "Libby washed these for you. Now be careful riding home, all right?"

"I will."

The three of them left, with Tom shooting her a hopeful glance as he went out the door last.

"See you tomorrow," he said.

Joy lifted her hand, wishing she could look forward to their date as much as he seemed to.

She took the scrunchie out of her hair and sat in a chair, running her fingers through the long waves to straighten out some of the kinks. With an obliging clank, the dishwasher started to hiss, which meant it was draining. Just a few more minutes.

And then she'd be free to leave.

She propped her head in her hand and stared across the expanse of the kitchen. Her mind raced. What was Gray doing now? Was he slipping in between cool sheets, pulling that woman's warm body to his?

"You look exhausted."

She jumped.

Gray's voice was vaguely accusatory. As if he were upset she didn't take better care of herself.

Like her health was any of his business, she thought.

"I'm only waiting for the dishwasher and then I'm leaving."

He went over to a window. "Didn't you come on a bike?"

"I did."

Gray frowned. "You can't go home on one at this hour."

"Oh, yes, I can."

"No, you can't."

"I beg your pardon?" She glared at him and knotted up her hair.

As he stared back, his face was fierce. God, with his dark hair and those narrow, pale eyes, he looked kind of scary.

"I'll give you a ride home."

"No, thanks." She got off the chair, went over to the dishwasher and yanked out the tray of pots even though the cycle wasn't all the way finished. She began to unload them onto the counter even though they burned her hands.

When a response didn't come back at her, she glanced over her shoulder. He was gone.

She let out her breath.

Thank God he'd given up.

She quickly put the dirty glasses in the washer's tray, slid the load in and hit the switch. It took her two minutes in the bathroom to change into her own clothes and leave the waitress uniform on the counter. On her way out, she looked around for the light switch that controlled the big fixtures hanging from the ceiling. She didn't want to waste a lot of time, though, so she turned off the ones she could before putting the back door to good use.

Gray was leaning against the side of the house, arms crossed over his thick chest. Right next to her bike.

"Let's go," he said, picking the thing up as if it weighed no more than a plate.

"Put that down!"

"Make me."

Yeah, like that was going to happen. He was only a foot taller than she and he had the bike up on his shoulder. Short of kicking him a good one in the knee, a line she wasn't prepared to cross, that man could do anything he wanted with her property.

"I don't like bullies," she said through gritted teeth.

"And I don't care if you like me or not."

Ouch. For some reason, that hurt.

She stared at him as he started walking off and then she realized he was headed for the lake, not the garage behind his house.

He wasn't going to throw the bike in the water, was he?

Joy ran after him. "That's my property! You can't just toss it—"

Gray glanced over his shoulder. "It'll be easier to put this thing in my boat than jam it into the back of my car."

As he strode along, she nearly had to jog to keep up with him.

If she wasn't mistaken, he seemed almost as eager as she was to part company.

GRAY COULD FEEL JOY'S EYES shooting into his back. She was right royally pissed and he was a little surprised. He never expected she'd put up a fight about anything. Not Joy. Not sweet, strawberry-blonde Joy.

Damn, but her unexpected strength was attractive. It wasn't going to change his mind, but he admired anyone who tried to stand up to him.

And he didn't care if he had to throw her over his other shoulder, she was not going home alone in the dark on that bike. The godforsaken thing didn't even have a headlight and the fact that there wasn't a lot of traffic in the area off-season didn't matter to him. Cars weren't the only hazard on the Lake Road. Black bears came down to the shore looking for food in the fall. Mountain lions, too.

So no, he wasn't about to let her be meals-on-wheels for some rabid, claw-wielding animal.

He opened the door to the boathouse and flipped on the light. The Hacker gleamed in its slip, all that glossy mahogany and shiny chrome reflecting the illumination like a prism. He put the bike in one of the seating compartments and then stepped on the gunnels, offering Joy a hand. When she refused to take it, he let her get settled on her own.

Getting in beside her, he started the engine. A great thunder filled the boathouse before the RPMs settled down to a rhythmic, almost sexual pump.

God, he really was hard up for her, wasn't he? He'd driven the Hacker for years and never found anything erotic in it.

As soon as they were free of the boathouse, he pulled a blanket from under the dash and gave it to her. She looked at the thing as if it were a net and she was a fish.

"It's cold," he said dryly.

She took the heavy wool from him and spread the tartan plaid over her body. "What about you?"

He shrugged, enjoying the chill because it kept him sharp. He'd only had those two bourbons all night long, but it wasn't the alcohol that was likely to get him doing something stupid. "I'll live."

A moment later she shifted in the seat. "You could speed us up and get this over with, you know. We're barely going faster than an idle."

"Less wind this way." Which was a crock. He liked having her in his boat.

She cursed softly. And then slid over next to him, awkwardly pulling the blanket over his lap. Her hand brushed against his stomach.

Gray closed his eyes, body humming like he had jet fuel in his veins.

When they'd been collecting glasses in the library, and she'd stopped short, he hadn't been prepared for the abrupt halt. One minute they were making good progress around the room. And the next, his erection was pressed up against her.

Remembering the feel of her made a groan rise in his throat and he was grateful for the sound of the engine.

He'd been watching her as she'd moved, the swaying of her hips, the shifting of her shoulders. Her legs were long and slender, and every time she bent this way or that, the skirt had ridden up a little higher on her thighs.

At the moment they'd come into contact, he'd been picturing himself putting the tray aside, sitting her down on one of the leather couches and parting her legs with his hands. He'd wanted to fall to his knees and kiss his way up the inside of her thighs. Feel her hands burrowing deep into his hair as she urged him closer to her heat. The image had been hot, wild, totally insane.

Yeah, and then he'd bumped into her.

She must have felt what she did to him. How could she have missed it?

And if it hadn't been clear then, it must have been obvious when she'd wheeled around. He'd known his lust was showing on his face, but everything had happened so fast, the meeting of their bodies followed by her quick spin, that he hadn't been able to strong-arm his expression into any semblance of neutrality.

No wonder she didn't want to be alone with him.

Maybe that was why he was so hell-bent on taking her home. He wanted to prove to them both that he could take care of her. Because back in that library, he sure hadn't been thinking like Gallahad and she'd caught him red-handed.

Or red-blooded, as the case had been.

Gray felt something tickle his face. A strand of her

hair had escaped the loose knot at her neck and was dancing in the wind. He reached for the silken length, but she caught it first and tucked it behind her ear.

"Sorry," she said.

He wasn't. He wanted her hair down and all over his body.

Gray reached up and massaged the bridge of his nose.

"Are you okay?" she said gruffly, as if she didn't like being concerned for him. "You look like you're really cold or something."

No, he wasn't cold. He could have jumped buck-naked into an ice bath and had the damn thing boiling in a matter of minutes.

"Gray?"

"I'm fine." Yup, for a guy being tortured by his libido, he was just Jim-dandy.

He took his hand off the steering wheel and gave the throttle a push to speed them up. She might have a point about getting the ride over with.

"Your father seemed to enjoy himself tonight."

"He did."

There was a pause. "He looks better than when you and he ate at White Caps last month."

"He's coming along. It's been hard for him."

"And you, too, I imagine. I, ah, I saw how carefully you watched him tonight."

The words were soft. He looked at her.

Joy was staring out at the lake.

"How's your brother doing?" he asked, thinking she must know all about how tough it was to see someone suffer through rehab and recovery.

"He had another operation two weeks ago. They replaced his tibia with a titanium rod and he still might need to go back under the knife again. They're not sure. He's also been struggling with a post-op infection." She pulled up the edge of the blanket and began braiding the fringe. "He's been so brave. He never complains even though it's obvious he's in a great deal of pain. I think the hardest thing for us is the fact that he's a terrible patient. He won't take his meds a lot of the time. He drinks too much. And he never talks about what happened."

Gray wanted to reach out for her hand.

"I'm really sorry," he said instead.

Her eyes came to his face. "Thank you."

"You take care of your grandmother, don't you?"

"Yes."

"That's a lot of responsibility."

Joy shrugged. "No one would tend to her as well as I'm able to. And she really can't be alone. The dementia has taken away most of her internal logic and reasoning and replaced them with paranoia. We're trying her on a new medication right now and I hope it calms her. I hate to see her distressed."

"You're a very good person, Joy," he said abruptly.

She shrugged. "Alex and Grand-Em are my family. Of course I'd take care of them."

"There's no 'of course' about it." His mother had had no compunction about letting others worry about him. Hell, when he'd contracted viral pneumonia in first grade, and had spent two weeks in a pediatric intensive care unit trying to breathe, he'd seen the woman only once. "They're fortunate to have you care so much."

Joy looked away. They were quiet for a while, but some of the tension had been eased.

It wasn't until White Caps came into view that he broke the silence.

"I'm sorry about what happened tonight."

She gave a short laugh. "This boat ride hasn't been too hard to endure."

"No, in the library."

Joy stiffened. "Oh, that."

Yeah, *that.*

"I'm glad Cassandra came in when she did," he muttered, replaying the scene in his head and having to shift in his seat.

"So am I." Her voice had an edge.

So he had offended her, he thought.

Gray cleared his throat. "I don't want you to think that I'd ever…take advantage of a woman."

"Believe me, I don't," she said dryly.

As he pulled into the dock, he knew she was angry again, but he didn't regret making the apology. It had been the right thing to do.

He threw a rope around a cleat to keep the boat in place and then lifted out her bike. He wanted to say something else, but she didn't give him the chance.

"I can take that up," she said quickly. "Thanks for the ride."

And without a backward glance, she rushed away, the wheels of her bike bumping along the dock planks.

He watched her until she was all the way up to the house, heading around the corner, disappearing out of sight.

He had an absurd impulse to run after her.

But then what?

Then he would take her into his arms and pull her so

close that he'd feel every breath she took. And he'd kiss her until neither one of them could stand up.

Get in this boat, he told himself. And go home, Bennett.

It was another ten minutes before he could make himself leave.

JOY MARCHED UP the lawn, grip tight on the bars of her bike.

God, he'd *apologized.*

How humiliating was that? As if she needed the confirmation that what he'd been feeling had had nothing to do with her. Sure he'd been happy to see Cassandra! Happier still, no doubt, to hear she was heading for bed. Because he'd clearly been thinking of the redhead when he'd become…well, *aroused.*

And of course, he didn't take advantage of women. A man like him didn't have to, because who would turn him down? God, as much as she hated to admit it, she wouldn't have. If he'd reached out to her, she would have stepped right into his arms and opened herself up to him, even though he'd had another woman in his mind.

Could the situation with him get any worse? she wondered. Her fantasies had been bad enough, but now she actually knew what his body felt like.

Okay, so it had only been for a second, but the impression was indelible.

And the idea he was going home to put that hard length of his to good use was a total nightmare.

She squeezed her eyes shut.

Her date with Tom tomorrow night was a godsend.

It really was. Honestly. She needed to try to connect with someone she could actually—

The toe of her shoe caught a tree root and she pitched forward. Dropping the bike and pinwheeling her arms, she managed to recover her balance before she face-planted into a pachysandra bed. But absurdly, tears pricked her eyes.

She wanted to curse.

Except she didn't know why meeting Gray's lover should bother her so much. The man was completely out of her league and she knew it. He was sophisticated and urbane and…she was a virgin, for heaven's sake.

Joy put her hands over her face, wincing at her own inexperience. It wasn't that she hadn't had boyfriends. There had been a few, back in high school. But when college had rolled around, she'd had to work to help pay her way. The guys she'd met then were into partying and having fun. Between her course load and her two jobs, she'd been exhausted most of the time and not exactly the poster girl for a happy-go-lucky relationship. And as soon as she'd graduated, she'd come home to take care of Grand-Em. Saranac Lake was a small community so there weren't a lot of eligible guys her own age to date. Besides, taking care of Grand-Em was an around-the-clock kind of job.

So how was she supposed to have found a man she really wanted to be with?

God, she was a fossil. At the age of twenty-six, she was a total fossil.

Joy dropped her hands and glanced up at the sky. The stars overhead were blurry.

She should have known right off the bat that the night was going to end badly.

Getting hit with a tortellini air raid the minute she'd walked into the man's house could not be, *had not been,* a harbinger of good things.

As she forced herself to pick up the bike and start walking, she thought at least one prediction of hers had come true. She wasn't going to get any sleep tonight.

So she might as well get back to work on her sister's wedding gown.

CHAPTER FOUR

THE NEXT MORNING, Joy threw down her pincushion as Frankie tore out of the bedroom. In the wedding gown.

"Frankie! Wait, you can't—"

"I have to catch Stu before he leaves! His phone is out."

Joy leaped to her feet and ran after her sister, figuring at least she could grab the skirting and keep it off the ground. Assuming she could catch up. When she finally got within range, Frankie was flying out the kitchen door. Together, they hightailed it for Stu's produce truck.

Wiry, ancient Stu was about to get in the cab, John Deere cap pulled down low, coveralls hanging off him like a sack. The old man was a typical Adirondack woodsman. Which meant if he was surprised to see Frankie coming at him in a wedding gown, you'd never know it.

"Nate and Spike need a special delivery of arugula," Frankie said breathlessly. "Is there any way—"

"Yup."

"By Tuesday?"

"Yup."

"Stu, you are a magician! Thank you."

There was a pause. "Yup."

Stu doffed his cap and climbed up into the truck.

Just as he was about to take off, a car came down the driveway.

It was a big BMW. Gray's.

Joy nearly dropped the dress, at least until the lovely redhead got out. Then she began squeezing the fabric in her fists. She dropped the skirting before she got it sweat stained.

Frankie lifted a hand in greeting. "Good morning."

"Hi." Cassandra smiled in a small, tight way, as if she were uncomfortable. But then her eyes narrowed on the gown. "Good Lord, that's marvelous."

Frankie did a twirl. The white satin skirt billowed out as if the fabric knew it was time to show off. "Isn't it?"

"Who's it by? Narciso Rodriguez? No, Michael Kors."

"Her." Frankie pointed at Joy.

Cassandra's eyes widened. "You did this?"

Joy nodded.

The redhead walked around Frankie, inspecting seams and folds. "You designed and made it yourself?"

"It's a hobby."

"You're very good. Do you have any others?"

"Gowns? No. Designs? Tons of them. I could wallpaper the house with what I've sketched."

"You're quite good." Cassandra smiled more widely, but the expression faded as she looked at Frankie. "I probably should have called first. I, uh, I was hoping Alex would see me."

Frankie nodded. "Come on in. I'll let him know you're here."

As they walked over to the kitchen door, Cassandra smiled at Joy. "And maybe afterward, you could show me some more of your work?"

Joy shrugged as they went inside, figuring the woman was just being polite. "I was refining a few sketches this morning during breakfast. They're over here on the table."

Cassandra went right to them and her focus was so intense, it was intimidating.

Joy sank down in a chair, wishing she hadn't been so quick to offer up her work. No one but her family had ever seen her designs. And here was a woman dressed in an Escada jacket and slacks pouring over an amateur's pathetic scratchings. Joy wanted to grab the drawings. Hide them. Protect them.

Cassandra went through the loose pile, sliding the thick sheets one on top of another. Joy wanted to point out errors, mistakes, places where she thought she could do better. But she couldn't find her voice.

Besides, no doubt Cassandra would find the faults herself.

The woman looked up.

Please don't be cruel, Joy thought. Let me down softly.

"These are wonderful," the woman said, glancing back to the sketches. "You have an old-fashioned approach, particularly in the bodices, but the total effect comes across as fresh. Your color combinations are vivid and the elegance of line is…masterful."

Joy went a little dizzy.

Cassandra smiled and looked across the table with open, friendly eyes. "You're quite good. Perhaps better than good. Where did you go to school?"

"UVM."

"I didn't know they had a design program."

"I majored in business."

The redhead frowned. “Then who taught you this?”

“Well…I suppose my grandmother’s ballgowns and day suits from the fifties. She wore Mainboucher, St. Laurent. Chanel, of course. I’ve deconstructed all of her clothes. Taken them apart, laid them out panel by panel, studied how the structure of the garment was created in the seams and the folds and the gathers. Then I’ve stitched them back together. She wears them still. She’s—she’s ill, and if she doesn’t look her best, the dementia gets worse. We can’t afford new ones of the quality she once had so I just learned how to patch and preserve. In the process, I guess I got an education.”

“How extraordinary.” There was respect and compassion in Cassandra’s voice.

Well, this was just terrible, Joy thought.

First the woman turns up on Gray’s arm. Then she turns out to be a nice person.

God, as petty as it was, it would somehow be easier to dislike the widow.

Frankie came down the stairs, flushed as if she’d been in an argument.

“I’m sorry, Cassandra. He’s not awake.”

“He doesn’t want to see me, you mean,” the woman said in a small voice.

“I’m so sorry.”

Cassandra shook her head. “I’m sure it’s too raw for him still. Thank you for trying.”

“He’s just…” Frankie’s mouth thinned. “He’s hardened so much, he won’t listen to anyone.”

“Don’t be angry with him. I’m sure he’s doing the best he can.”

“Yeah, well, he won’t heal if he doesn’t let people in.”

“That’s his choice.” Cassandra took a deep breath.

"But I shouldn't be telling you what to do about your own brother."

"You're the only one outside of the family who has any right to an opinion," Frankie said quietly. "I know I said it last night, but I'm so sorry for…everything you lost."

"Thank you." Cassandra's eyes closed briefly. And then as if she were pulling herself out of a spiral, she looked at the table. "These sketches are truly wonderful, Joy. You have a spectacular eye."

After goodbyes were exchanged, Joy and Frankie stood in the kitchen doorway and watched the BMW go around the bend in the driveway.

"I really liked her," Joy said, heading back to the kitchen table. Her papers were in an orderly pile now. After Cassandra had looked at them, the woman had been careful to gather the drawings together, stacking one on top of the other. As if they were art.

"She is lovely," Frankie said. "And she liked your stuff."

Joy rifled through her work, looking at the images with fresh eyes.

"What time is Tom picking you up?" Frankie asked.

"What? Oh, seven. And thanks for watching Grand-Em for me."

"My pleasure. It's been too long since you've been out of this house and Tom's a—"

"Really nice guy. I know. You've told me that." And Joy knew it too well.

"There's nothing to be defensive about," Frankie said gently. "What's going on, Joy? Are you nervous?"

"No. Not really. Now let's get you out of that dress,

okay? I'm living in terror of the grass stains you may have gotten on the skirt."

"Are you sure you're not worried about tonight? It's been a while since you've gone on a date."

"Thanks for the reminder." Joy winced at her sharp tone. Biting her sister's head off wasn't normally something she did, but being reminded that she was going to be alone with Tom made her feel raw.

Probably because he wasn't the guy she wished she was having dinner with and she felt badly about that. And also because she couldn't have the man she wanted.

Neither of which was her sister's fault.

"Sorry. I take that back, Frankie."

"It's okay. I suppose I just want you to have what I found."

Joy took her sister's hand. "That's because you've always sought the best for me and you're totally in love with a great guy. But maybe that kind of thing's not in store for me, you know? And if it isn't, that's okay. Come on. Out of that dress."

But it wasn't okay. Not really. Somehow going on a date with a nice guy she really *should* like made her feel lonely. But Frankie was right. Even if Tom wasn't the man she was going to end up married to, Joy needed to get out of the house.

Although by the time six-thirty rolled around, she almost had to cancel. Grand-Em was all worked up because she'd misplaced her first edition copy of *Jane Eyre*. The trouble was, she'd lost the book in 1963 while traveling abroad. Frankie insisted on handling the crisis so Joy could get ready and all was eventually calmed when Grand-Em took to reading the operating instructions for the new backup generator they'd bought.

The relief Joy felt when it looked as if she might have an out seemed like an insult to Tom so she became determined to make an extra effort. While blow-drying her hair, she talked to herself about giving people a chance, seeing past the obvious, valuing the steady over the exciting and dangerous. She even tried to channel various fairy tales with happy endings. The trouble with that, though, was Gray kept showing up in the prince suit with the glass slipper in his hand.

When Tom's pickup rambled up to the house, she went downstairs, said goodbye to Frankie and Nate, and headed outside.

Tom came around and opened the door for her. He was freshly showered, wearing a button-down shirt that was painfully free of wrinkles. His khakis were likewise right off the ironing board. He looked like a man who had taken special care with his clothes and was uncomfortable in them, either because of all the effort he'd gone to or because he wished he had better options.

"You know what I think we should do?" he said as he got behind the wheel. "There's a concert in the square tonight. They're serving barbecue. We could walk around, listen to the music, eat on the grass."

"That'd be great."

He put the truck in gear and looked across the seat at her. "You look really pretty, Joy."

She closed her eyes and took a deep breath. She smelled Windex, as if he'd cleaned the cab for her. "Thanks, Tom."

GRAY PARKED THE BMW in front of Barclay's Liquors, taking a space as it was vacated by a minivan. The town square was hopping tonight. A couple of white tents covered about half of the two-acre stretch of grass. Underneath them, people sat at picnic tables, eating barbecue that was being cooked over open flames on big, flat grills. In between the tents, a twenty-piece swing band was set up in Saranac Lake's signature Victorian gazebo, its righteous horn section ripping through a Count Basie standard. People were dancing on a parquet floor lit with torches.

"Does the town do this often?" Cassandra asked as they crossed the street.

"Once a month or so in the summer. This must be the last one. In another couple weeks, it's going to be too cold."

Three teenage girls skittered by wearing glow-in-the-dark, green neon necklaces. In their rush, they moved over the ground with the same restless excitement and chatter as the loose, colorful leaves swirling in the chilly wind. The sound of their laughter made Gray smile as he and Cass ambled over to the tents. Smoke, infused with molasses and cayenne pepper, drifted into his nose. His stomach checked in with a grumble of approval.

"When are you going back to D.C.?" Cassandra asked.

"Very soon. I need to go to New York next week and then I'll move Papa down."

"Are you teaching that poli-sci seminar at Columbia again this semester?"

"Yeah. They asked me back."

"We'll have to have dinner. Maybe Allison and Roger can join us."

"Sounds good," Gray replied, even though the thought of the Adamses made him wince. He still couldn't believe the adultery story, and was hoping when he looked into the facts Beckin had given him, that it would all be just a bunch of B.S.

As he and Cass stopped in front of the band, he glanced over at her. She was staring at the couples that were dancing. "You ready for some food or do you want to risk a little swinging with me?"

"Sounds good."

"Let's try eating first," he said gently. Cassandra had been remote since going to see Alex Moorehouse. Gray gathered that the meeting hadn't gone well, but she didn't seem to want to talk about it so he didn't press.

As they got in line, he looked over at the people in front of the band. There were a couple of folks who could really dance, the men swinging the women over their shoulders, twirling their dates or wives around in circles. There was one couple who were damn good. The guy handled his woman as though she were an extension of his own body and she responded to him as if thinking of the same move at the same time he did.

Gray stopped moving.

Good Lord, it was Joy.

As the song came to a fevered end, that White Caps cook spun her around, flipped her over his back and then dipped her low, holding her in place. Joy hung on to his shoulders, head back, breathlessly laughing. Her hair drifted down, almost touching the floor as she looked up at her partner.

Young and free. So beautiful, she hurt Gray's eyes.

The man slowly lifted her to the vertical, his hands lingering on the small of her back.

Gray ground his teeth. He had a stupid, near overwhelming urge to march across the dance floor and peel the other guy off her. Roughly. And sure enough, he felt his weight shifting to his left foot and his right knee bending up. As if his body were not under his control.

He forced himself to look away.

Her boyfriend had every right to touch her. And given the way she'd held on to him during that flashy finale, she wanted the guy's hands on her.

Damn it.

"Gray? What's the matter?"

Evidently he'd spoken out loud. "Nothing."

"We're up. What do you want?"

Now if that wasn't a loaded question.

When they'd gone through the line, they took their food over to a picnic table and squeezed in with a couple and their two kids.

Gray bit into a steaming rib. Spicy and piping hot from the grill, the burn on his lips and tongue was distracting, but didn't go far enough.

Then again, he'd need someone to go Medieval on his ass to get Joy off his mind.

"So tell me something," Cassandra said as she picked up a piece of chicken, her pinkies cocked.

"Hmm?"

"How long have you wanted her?"

Gray froze.

Okay. So now his pork tasted like an old shoe.

"What the hell are you talking about?"

"Don't play dumb with me, Bennett. I saw how you were looking at Joy just now. And last night."

Gray stabbed some coleslaw with his plastic fork. Thought about putting the subject on ice. Didn't.

"You see that guy with her? The young one?"

Cassandra nodded.

"You see how happy he makes her?"

"I see how much she enjoys the dancing. I don't know how much of it is him."

Gray leveled his eyes across the picnic table. "Don't split hairs. She's glowing. You honestly think I could make her feel that way?"

"Well, yes."

"Wrong. A girl like that is going to want more than sex, Cass. Hell, she deserves more than that. And flyboy with the smooth moves over there no doubt has love on his tongue and a ring in his pocket. A couple of nights is all I can offer her. Maybe not even that."

"Don't shortchange yourself."

"You know my history and people don't change."

"Not true."

He rolled his eyes and poked at his food. "Fine. I'm not going to change. She's not my type and I like her too much to—"

"Hi, Gray. Cassandra."

His head snapped up. Joy and the cook were walking by the table.

As she lifted her hand in a tentative greeting, Gray's eyes went over every inch of her black sweater and her worn blue jeans. Her hair had curled up around her face from exertion and her cheeks were flushed.

Oh, sweet, beautiful girl, he thought, fingers tightening on his plastic fork until it bent in two. He dropped the thing quickly and wiped his mouth.

"Hey, Joy," he said before hitting the blond-haired guy by her side with what he hoped passed for pleasant inquiry. "Tom, right?"

Tom nodded slowly, as if he sensed he should tread carefully. "Yes, Mr. Bennett."

"Gray. Call me Gray. Any friend of Joy's is a friend of mine."

Tom's eyes narrowed as if he didn't believe a word of it.

Smart kid, Gray thought.

Cassandra rushed in, as if she, too, had picked up on Gray's latent aggression. "We were just watching you on the dance floor."

"Tom's much better than I am," Joy said, smiling at the guy. "But he's teaching me."

"And she learns fast."

Gray felt his eyes go into a full squint and had to remind himself that he had no right to be jealous. Possessive. Resentful.

Although, man, that urge to step in between the two of them was back with a vengeance. All he wanted to do was to throw Joy over his shoulder and take her as far away from the bastard Opie look-alike as he could carry her.

Which would be Canada, he thought. Or maybe Alaska.

As Joy and the boyfriend left, Gray picked up a rib and cleaned the meat off the bone with relish.

"Gray, if she's not your type, why do you stare at her like that?"

"Because I'm an idiot. You want more barbecue? I'm getting seconds."

CHAPTER FIVE

"SO WHERE'D YOU LEARN to dance like that?" Joy asked as she and Tom sat down with their plates. Now that the band had taken a break, it was easier to talk.

"I took lessons when I was living in Albany. My old girlfriend made me go, but then I really liked it."

"You're wonderful."

"Thanks."

As they tucked into their barbecue, Joy looked over at the table where Gray and Cassandra were sitting. Gray was frowning and shaking his head as he got to his feet with his empty plate. He was taller than most everyone, so tracking him through the crowd was easy.

He'd looked so fierce when she'd gone over to say hello. Sure, he was never the kind of man who came across as easygoing, but something about him seemed extra sharp tonight.

"I'm glad you asked me out," Tom said.

She glanced across the table. Tom wasn't looking at her. He was pushing some coleslaw around his plate, his mouth drawn.

She took a deep breath. "Tom, I—"

"You don't have to say it, Joy. I know. Just friends." He smiled into his food, as if he hoped she'd buy the no-big-deal expression as long as he hid his eyes from her. "It's okay. You don't have to feel badly. We've had fun tonight."

"I honestly had hoped…"

"Me, too." Now he looked at her. "But I don't want you to worry. I'm not going to go all weird on you or anything. When you see me around the kitchen, it'll be just like before."

She shook her head. "It is quite possible, Tom Reynolds, that you are the nicest guy on the planet."

"Yeah, well, keep it to yourself. Women seem to prefer the tough ones."

"Never could figure that one out," she murmured, watching Gray return to his table with a full plate. She had to make herself look away from his wide shoulders and his long arms.

Tom wiped his hands on a paper napkin, shredding it. "I think it's a fact of nature. Women are drawn to strength. Which is why you want him like you do."

Her eyes popped.

"Come on, Joy. It's so obvious and it's not one-sided. That Bennett man was ready to take my throat in his hand when we walked by his table. Just be careful. Underneath all that breeding and money, there's something scary hard about him."

Joy glanced back at Gray and Cassandra. Two people had come up to them and Cassandra was nodding and picking up her plate. Gray seemed grim as he did the same.

They headed right for Joy and Tom.

Joy slowly put down her fork.

Oh, please be going for the trash bins, she thought.

"Hi," Cassandra said. "May we join you? Our table wants the rest of their family to sit with them and I figured Gray and I might as well find some people we know."

"Sure," Joy said.

Gray sat down next to Tom. The men nodded to each other and then settled into eating. Neither looked happy.

Cassandra smiled. "You know, Joy, I really liked your designs today. I've been thinking about them all afternoon."

"What kind of designs?" Gray asked.

Joy stayed quiet, thinking the last thing the man needed was to hear about her hobby. But Cassandra filled the silence.

"Dresses. She makes dresses. Evening gowns, actually. And they're fantastic."

"I didn't know that."

"It's just a thing I do," Joy said, avoiding his eyes.

"I was wondering," Cassandra said, "do you accept commissions?"

"Commissions?"

"If I asked you to make a dress for me, would you do it?"

Joy stared at the woman. "Why would you want me to do that?"

"Because you're good."

She eyed Cassandra's Chanel jacket. "The kind of designers you can afford are better."

Cassandra shrugged and took out a business card. "If you'd rather not, that's fine. But call me if you're interested."

The band filed back on to the gazebo's stage and began tuning up.

"Tom," Cassandra said. "Could you show me how to swing dance? If Joy wouldn't mind, of course."

Tom looked at Joy. "Is it okay with you?"

"Absolutely," she said.

Tom glanced hesitantly at Gray, as if the other man might put up a protest. When Gray just picked up another rib, Tom got to his feet and disappeared with the redhead into the crowd.

In the long silence that followed, Joy tried to find some distraction. Unfortunately the band's cheerful music, the laughter from the other tables, the shouts of children who were weaving in and out of the crowd, none of it offered anything half so interesting as Gray's brooding presence.

"You're crazy not to," he said.

"What?"

"Design something for Cass." He cleaned the meat off another rib with his teeth and then licked his lips.

Abruptly, Joy felt like taking her sweater off. Even though it was in the fifties.

Gray picked up a napkin and went to work on his hands. "She's a trendsetter in New York. If you ever wanted to get noticed, this is the way to do it."

"I don't know if I want to get noticed," she murmured.

He smiled slowly, as if that pleased him. Although God only knew why. She'd assume a man like him would only be impressed by killer instincts.

"You want to dance?" he asked, meeting her in the eye.

Definitely time to lose the sweater, she thought.

"I don't think—"

"I'll tell you up front. I'm not as good as Tom. Not even close. But I know enough to stay off your feet."

Eyes remote, he stood up. Extended his hand. And waited.

More contact with him was exactly what she didn't need.

So she cursed her lack of self-control as she got to her feet. And the moment she put her palm against his, naturally, the band slipped into the old Sinatra ballad, "Three Coins In The Fountain."

"Maybe we should wait until they speed it up," Joy said. His hand was big. Warm. Steady.

"Probably." His voice was low as he led her over to the band. "We probably should."

She was dimly aware that Tom and Cassandra were walking off the dance floor, heading toward the make-it-yourself sundae bar. As the remaining couples started getting close, Joy went blank on the whole slow dance thing. Just stood there with her arms down and her eyes on the band.

As if she could will them into playing a fricking polka.

In a smooth movement, Gray stepped up to the plate and took charge, which was embarrassing. He lifted both her hands up to his shoulders and rested his own on her waist. His body began to move. Hers followed instinctively.

And she became aware of every inch of him.

His muscles were hard beneath her hands as they shifted under his sports jacket.

She couldn't look him in the eye so she focused on the tanned skin of his neck. And the way his dark hair brushed the top of his shirt collar. And the strength of the hands that held her firmly and with total confidence.

He would know what to do with a woman's body,

she thought. How to stroke it. How to kiss it. How to make a woman moan.

God, he smelled good.

One of his hands moved to the small of her back. Nudged her a little closer to him.

She glanced up. His pale blue eyes were hooded and in the dim light of the tent she couldn't read his expression.

"I didn't want that person to bump into you," he explained, nodding over her head.

Oh, right. Of course.

He let the space grow back between them. And she meant to look away, she really did. The trouble was, her eyes got stuck on his lips.

His mouth was so close to hers. Only a matter of some inches. All she'd have to do to kiss him would be to go up on her tiptoes and lean forward. Then she would know what he tasted like.

"Joy." His voice was stern. "Look at me, Joy."

"Huh?" She lifted her eyes.

"Hello," he said sarcastically.

She frowned. "What's wrong?"

"I wanted you to remember who you're dancing with."

As if she could forget. "Believe me, I'm not likely to get you and Tom confused."

"Then stop staring at my mouth like you're hungry. Save those looks for your boyfriend."

Joy's face burned. "I don't know what you are talking about."

Liar, liar, pants on fire, she thought.

Gray cursed. "The hell you don't. And get your hand off my neck."

Joy jerked the thing back, wondering how it had wandered from the socially acceptable position on his shoulder up to his nape.

"Man, I've got to hand it to Tom."

"What?"

Gray's hands tensed on her waist. And then his head bent down. His voice was deep and a little hoarse as it vibrated in her ear.

"Do you have any idea what those eyes of yours can do to a man?"

Joy stopped breathing. Nearly stopped moving. The music, the people, the tent, the whole world faded away. The only thing she knew was the raw male heat vibrating out of Gray's big body. She looked up. His eyes held the promise of naked skin on naked skin. Of dangerous, emotionally reckless sex that would break her heart into a thousand pieces.

"Damn it, Joy. You're killing me."

She stayed quiet, lost in his eyes.

"Fair warning," he gritted out. "I'm about to show you just what that look's doing to me. And you weren't too crazy about feeling it last night, remember?"

"That's because you were thinking about someone else."

"Was I?" Gray made a low sound in his throat and pulled her closer. Their thighs brushed. His palms moved up her rib cage and he flexed his fingers as though he was testing the strength of her bones. As though he wanted to crush her against him.

But then she was put back impersonally. Almost as if she were an inanimate object like salt and pepper shakers or a phone he was through using.

She was disappointed until she met his eyes. They burned.

"Goddamn, I hope Tom knows how lucky he is," Gray muttered.

"It's not like that."

"How old is he?" As if Gray hadn't even heard her.

"Twenty-nine."

His eyes assumed a bored look. "Perfect age for you."

She thought about pointing out, again, that she and Tom weren't together. But then it might seem as if she were sending Gray a message, and she had her pride. Besides, the song was over and he was already pulling away.

They went back to the table where Tom and Cassandra were chatting over the remnants of their sundaes. The redhead stood up.

"This has been such fun," she said, "but I need to leave early tomorrow to go back to the city. Tom, it was great to meet you…."

As the goodbyes started rolling, Joy glanced at Gray. He was smiling at something Cassandra had said and shaking Tom's hand.

It was the middle of September, she thought. He would be leaving soon to go back to his real life and he wouldn't return to Saranac for months and months. Whole seasons would have to pass, the chilly autumn and the bitter winter and the wet, cold spring, before he would come back.

She carefully studied the planes of his face, noticing how his eyes creased at the corners as he smiled. How his five-o'clock shadow dusted his jaw. How his broad chest filled out his jacket. How his flat stomach led into his hips and then his long, long legs.

This was the last chance to see him until next summer.

And she was willing to bet she would never, ever, dance with him again.

Gray turned and looked at her. The smile slowly fell from his face.

"Goodbye, Joy."

She blinked quickly and lifted her chin, trying to be a grown-up. "'Bye, Gray. Have a good winter."

"Thanks. You, too."

And then he and Cassandra walked away, his hand on the small of her back as he helped her negotiate through the crowd.

"Joy?" Tom's voice was soft.

"Hmm? Sorry, what?" She looked at the ground, afraid the shine in her eyes would show in the torchlight.

"Would you like to go home now?" he said gently.

"Yes. Please." She picked up her plate and saw Cassandra's business card on the table.

Joy threw the thing out with the trash.

BACK AT HIS HOME, Gray undressed and got into bed naked.

He had an ache in his chest and rubbed his sternum. Damn barbecued ribs. He loved them, but man, he paid a price.

He dropped his hand onto the bedspread.

Ah, hell. Who was he kidding.

Joy had knocked him out tonight. Put him right on his ass.

That expression on her face, that uncalculated, sensual curiosity, had been like getting hit by a car. For a guy who knew all the plays in the female seduction handbook, direct, unreserved approaches were sexy as hell. But it wasn't just the novelty that got to him. His hot response was all about Joy. Her lavender scent. Her long, wavy hair. Her pale, smooth skin.

Just the memory of that dance had his body cranking up.

He punched his pillow, rolled over onto his side and shut his eyes.

It had taken some serious lecturing to convince his hands to stay on her waist. And preserving that two-inch distance between their bodies had made him shake.

Making her boyfriend the topic of conversation had seemed like the only way to break the mood. Otherwise he would have led her off the dance floor, past the tents and into the velvety darkness.

Where he would have been more than happy to indulge her appetite.

Indulge it until she was under him and hanging on for dear life as he…

His groan was pitiful and he thought of the nice guy she was with.

By the time Gray saw her next year, she could be engaged. Married.

What a lucky, lucky man that line cook was.

A WEEK LATER, Joy knocked on her brother's door. "Alex?"

She heard the sound of the bed creaking. Then a graveled voice. "Yeah?"

"Can I come in?"

"Hold on a sec."

As she waited, she took a deep breath.

"All right," Alex called.

She opened the door.

Alex was lying on the twin bed, his big body overflowing the mattress. His leg cast was elevated on a pillow and the one on his arm was tucked against his side. He'd obviously just pulled on a shirt because his hair was down flat on his forehead and he was tugging at the bottom hem.

In the past month he'd lost a lot of weight and it showed in his face. Harsh before, now the strong angles were drawn. And though a lot of his tan remained, the rich glow couldn't hide his gray pallor. His sun-streaked, dark hair was a mess, clean, but not combed.

"How are you?" she asked softly.

He frowned and ignored the question. "This isn't mealtime."

"No, it isn't." She looked for a place to sit in the sparse room. There was none, so she lowered herself to the floor next to his bed.

And went eye to eye with a half-empty Scotch bottle.

As she glanced at the liquor, Alex drummed his fingers on the mattress. He'd obviously had enough of Frankie's lectures to stop drinking. Eat all his food. Take his medicine.

"I need a favor," Joy asked. "Well, it's more than that."

The fingers stopped. "Okay."

But his suspicion was obvious in the way he dragged out the word.

"I, ah—" She paused, wishing there was another way to get what she needed. "Things are slowing down here now that we're closed for the season. Grand-Em's on that new medication and it seems to really be helping. Frankie's wedding's in good shape. Her dress is done."

Alex crossed his good arm over his chest. Even with everything the doctors had done to him, even though he'd dropped ten, maybe fifteen pounds, even though he was lying down, he was still imposing. "What do you need?"

"Cassandra Cutler's phone number."

There was a long silence. When Alex finally spoke, his voice was as tight as the tension in his jaw. "Mind if I ask why?"

"She saw some of my designs and asked me if I wanted to make a dress for her. I told her no, but…I don't know. I have some extra time and it might be kind of fun. The problem is, I threw out her business card and I don't know where she works. When I called information in Manhattan, her home phone's unlisted. I thought you might know how to get hold of her. I almost didn't want to ask because I don't want to upset you. In fact, if it makes you feel uncomfortable, I won't call her at all. I'll just let the whole thing go."

Alex pushed a hand through his hair. Closed his eyes.

"You know what?" Joy said. "This was a bad idea. I'm sorry—"

He shook his head. "No, it's no big deal. I'm glad someone's taken an interest in what you do and she's well known for that fashion thing."

He rattled off some numbers and she scrambled to find something to write them on.

"Say it again?" she said, scribbling on the back of a magazine.

"That's their apartment in New York."

"Thanks, Alex. This means a lot to me." Joy hesitated, eyeing the way the shirt sunk into his concave belly. "Can I bring you something to eat?"

"Don't start."

Joy glanced at the Scotch.

"And I really don't want to hear about the liquor."

Joy nodded. "Okay. I'll see you later when I bring up dinner."

"Don't hurry."

"Alex—"

"And shut the door tightly, will you?"

Joy left, wondering what she could do to help her brother and once again coming up with nothing.

Downstairs in Frankie's office, she felt somewhat foolish as she dialed the number Alex had given her. The person who picked up had a foreign accent that lengthened the words "Cutler residence" into a whole paragraph. After giving her name, Joy expected to get politely turned away when she asked to speak with Cassandra. Instead she was put on hold and then the widow came on the line.

"Joy! How nice to hear from you."

"I, uh, I've been thinking about what you said, about making a dress for you? And I'd like to, if you're still interested."

"Absolutely and your timing is perfect. The Hall Foundation is having its annual gala soon. When can you come to New York?"

New York City?

Good Lord. The last time she had been in a town bigger than Saranac was when she'd been in college. And Burlington, Vermont, wasn't exactly a towering metropolis of commerce. Heck, if a building had six stories there, it was considered a skyscraper.

"I can come anytime, I guess."

"Wonderful! Why don't you ride down tomorrow with Gray? He was supposed to come last week to teach his class at Columbia, but his father had some difficulties."

Oh, jeez. Four and a half hours in the car with Gray. One way.

And she thought the Big Apple was overwhelming. How was she going to keep sharp for that long?

"I—uh, maybe I should just take the train."

"Don't be silly. Gray will enjoy your company and he knows right where I live."

"Yeah, well—"

"Would you like me to call him for you?"

As if she didn't feel like enough of a rube already? "No. I'll do it."

"And you must stay with me. I have three guest rooms in this place that are rarely used. I could stand some company."

"That's really generous of you."

"My pleasure. See you tomorrow!"

Joy put the phone down and stared at it.

Now, she just had to call Gray.

GRAY LEANED FORWARD in the leather chair, planting his elbows on the desk.

"No, here's what you're going to tell your client. If he doesn't lay off, I'm going to crush him. Are we clear? Either the congressman cans the smear campaign against my boy, or I'm going to drop a dime to the *Boston Globe* and make sure the whole damn commonwealth knows what he tried to pull with those construction contracts. You remember, the ones he gave to his in-laws' shadow corporations?"

The lawyer on the other end of the line started to backpedal madly. As a heavy hitter sent in to intimidate, the guy had failed miserably. Gray was just too damn good at this kind of song and dance to be dressed down by nothing more than a big, loud noise with Esq. after its name.

Unfortunately, as November got closer, this backroom brawling stuff was only going to get more intense. He wasn't looking forward to all the threat trading. And he wasn't going to be thrilled to follow through on what he'd promised if the congressman's attack ads didn't dry up immediately.

Although he'd make the call in a heartbeat.

He reached for his bourbon. "Look, I've got to go. You're boring me."

Mr. Fancy Pants, Big City Attorney who'd tried to muscle in on the situation was still nattering as the line was cut.

Gray shook his head. What an amateur, trying to pull the whole legality of free speech nonsense. Sure there was the First Amendment and thank God for it. But the Constitution couldn't be used as a shield to protect liars. Not in Gray's world, anyway.

The phone rang.

Great. It was probably the lawyer again. Threatening to sue for tortuous interference of a phone call.

Gray picked up receiver and snapped, "What part of *bored* didn't you understand?"

There was a long silence.

"Gray?"

He put down the bourbon. “Hi—”

“It’s Joy Moorehouse.”

“Yeah, I know.”

“I, uh, I just got off the phone with Cassandra. I understand you’re going to New York City tomorrow and I was wondering if I could catch a ride with you.”

Gray took a deep breath. He hadn’t been aware of sending any requests to God lately. But evidently the Big Guy knew his stuff.

“Sure. I can pick you up. I’m leaving early, though. At seven.”

“Fine with me.”

“Are you going to do a dress for her?”

“Yes.”

“Good for you. And Cass.”

“So I guess I’ll see you in the morning.”

“Yeah. You will.”

Gray hung up. The tension that had crawled up his spine and burrowed into his shoulders while talking to the attorney slowly bled out of him.

Okay, so it was replaced with a state of half arousal. But anticipation, even if it was misplaced, misdirected and miserably persistent, was better than lawyer-onset annoyance any day.

Gray began to smile.

He tried to cover up the stupid grin by throwing back the bourbon and getting to work.

But the damn thing wouldn’t go away.

CHAPTER SIX

STANDING IN THE COOL morning air, with a small suitcase and her portfolio at her feet, Joy was totally disorientated. Surely she couldn't be going to New York City. In Gray's car. So she could talk about designing a dress for the man's überelegant lover.

The Twilight Zone tingles got more pronounced as the BMW came around the corner. When Gray got out, he greeted her with a smile.

"You ready?"

She did a quick survey of him. Dark suit. Bright tie. Crisp white shirt. Hair back and still a little damp. He smelled like cedar soap and that sophisticated, sandalwood aftershave he wore.

She reached for her luggage, but he got to the handles first, putting the suitcase and her drawings in the trunk. As she slid into the leather seat, she looked over and saw two stainless-steel coffee mugs.

"I brought some for you, too," he said as he got behind the wheel. "Wasn't sure how you liked yours so there's some sugar and cream in that bag at your feet."

Four hours later, Joy decided Einstein was right. Time was relative.

As the great city came into view and they got on Riverside Drive, she could have sworn she'd only been in the car for ten minutes. They talked the whole time.

Gray had been really interested in her designing. And the books she liked to read. And the music she listened to. And what she thought about a thousand different things, large and small. It was difficult not to fall even harder for him. Somehow, his curiosity in her was more attractive than his most attractive physical attributes.

And God knew the man was running a barn sale on tall, dark and handsome.

"Cass's place is on Park in the seventies," Gray said, as if that was supposed to mean something to her.

"I've never been here before."

"Really? You'll have to get her to show you around. New York is one of the best cities in the world. I love it here."

She looked out of the window. "It's…overwhelming."

The day was bright and clear, the buildings shooting up into a screaming blue, autumn sky. Everything seemed too sharp, especially the shadows thrown by the hard edges of so many skyscrapers. As vertigo taunted her stomach with threats of the bile variety, she brought her eyes back to level. No relief there. The blurring rush of pedestrians and taxis and trucks and bike couriers was like a carnival ride pregnant ladies weren't supposed to get on.

God, everyone looked as if they had somewhere they needed to be. Urgently. And the pace made the people seem important.

As her own internal tempo struggled to catch up, she wished she was back home at White Caps. It was just after eleven-thirty. She'd be getting Grand-Em's lunch ready. In the cozy familiarity of the kitchen. Using plates she'd put food on every day of her life.

What the hell was she doing in New York?

Taking a deep breath, she looked down at her lap to avoid all the visual stimulation. What she saw just made her feel smaller. She was wearing a pair of black slacks that had been cleaned so many times, the seams were a dark gray. There was only more of the same in her luggage. Lacking any clothes that were particularly chic, she'd stuffed her suitcase full of dark things in the hope that she'd look a little less like an upstate interloper.

She figured the Big Apple was not a place you wanted to hit in pastels. There was probably a city ordinance against pink. And forget about flower prints.

Except as she stared at the rushing people, she was certain no one would be fooled by her attempt at camouflage. Rubbing her palms on her thighs, she felt the cotton grab because her hands were sweaty.

"Do you get here often?" she asked, trying to distract herself.

Gray nodded. "I teach at Columbia every once in a while and I've got a couple of clients here. I usually end up coming in once, twice a month. Fortunately it's just a short plane ride from D.C."

"Do you have an apartment here?"

"I stay at the Waldorf Astoria Hotel."

She shifted in the bucket seat. Pulled at the collar of her black shirt.

"You okay?" Gray asked, glancing over at her.

"Yeah." She cleared her throat and tried again. "Yes, I am."

His hand reached across the seat. Covered one of hers briefly. And then returned to the wheel. "You're going to do fine."

She glanced over at him. He was focused on the

tangle of cabs and cars and trucks, but he was relaxed. With his bold profile, his tangible confidence, his well-made clothes, he seemed totally in control. Heck, he looked as if he had the power to clear the streets by a wave of his hand, but chose to endure the inconvenience of traffic because it was simply what a deity did if it lived among humans.

Had this man ever been scared? she thought. Lost? Sad?

Statistically speaking, the answer had to be yes. No one lived such a charmed life. But she just couldn't picture him vulnerable to anything.

"You're very lucky," she said softly.

Dark brows flickered. "Why?"

"Because you're so strong."

He frowned. "Trust me. Sometimes I'm not nearly strong enough."

Minutes later, Gray pulled up in front of a tall, pale building with a dark green awning. A uniformed doorman stepped forward and opened Joy's door.

"Mr. Bennett, how nice to see you again. Ma'am." The man tilted his cap.

"Rodney, how are you?" Gray popped the trunk and got her suitcase out. As he came up to her, he smoothly switched the luggage to his other hand when she tried to take it from him. "This is Joy Moorehouse. She's staying with Mrs. Cutler for the night. I'm just going to walk her upstairs."

Joy let herself get swept inside. The lobby was all marble floors and fresh bouquets of flowers, and the elevator was an old-fashioned brass-and-glass number that ran as if it were new. As they rode up, the chiming sound at each floor was cheerful.

When they came to a stop, Gray held the gate so she could step out first and then led her over to a single, ornate door in the hall. He rang the bell and a maid answered.

Cassandra wasn't far behind. "Oh, good! You're here in time for lunch. Gray, will you stay?"

He shook his head. "I've got to be at class in an hour. But are you both free for dinner tonight?"

Cass shook her head. "Allison and I are getting together, but I'm sure Joy would like to go out on the town, right?"

Joy glanced at Gray. "Don't feel as though you have to amuse me."

"I'll pick you up at seven."

And then he was gone.

JOY TAPPED HER PENCIL against the mahogany table and shook her head. She and Cassandra had been talking for hours.

"No, Cass, you're wrong. Red is the color you're going to want to wear and let me tell you why. If we go with the high-collared gown, we've got an opportunity to leverage your complexion and use it as part of the overall effect of the dress. The red will travel up your torso and frame your throat and jaw—see this line here? The color in concert with the design will set off your face like it was the inside of a flower. If you're uncomfortable, you can wear your hair up to lessen any contrast. But if I pick the right tone, and I will, you won't have to."

Joy waited, staring at the design she'd sketched out. She couldn't believe she was being so direct, but she was so sure of what she saw. She knew exactly what the gown would look like, what the color was going to be, how the satin would fall.

But she didn't want her first and only client to feel railroaded.

"I, uh, I'm sorry if I'm being pushy."

"Don't be." Cass looked up with a smile. "God, you are so much better than good. And you're absolutely right. Let's do it."

Joy tried not to beam. "You are not going to be sorry. I promise you."

A grandfather clock started to chime in the corner.

"Six o'clock," Cass said. "Gray will be here before you know it and I'm sure you'll want to get ready. By the way, the tub in your bathroom is perfect for soaking, or so I've been told by many a weary traveler."

As Joy started collecting her drawings, her sense of mastery dimmed. The reminder she was having dinner with Gray made her go back to feeling out of place.

And when her eyes flickered over the formal dining room, the alienation got sharper. Everything in it, from the heavy ivory drapes, to the Aubusson rug, to the dark oil paintings, had been chosen with a perfect sense of style. And a bottomless wallet. It had been so easy to forget that she and Cass were worlds apart when they'd been talking about designs.

But now reality was back.

"Joy?"

"Hmm?"

"There's nothing going on between Gray and me."

Joy's hands stilled. "That's none of my business."

"Maybe not, but I thought you'd want to know. Gray and I have been friends for years. He was one of my first clients when I got started as an architect." Cass picked up some of the colored pencils that were littering the table. "Would you mind if I pried a little?"

Joy shrugged, moving faster to gather her things. When her gum eraser popped out of her hand and made a swan dive for the floor, it was a relief to reach under the table.

"How long have you been interested in Gray?"

Joy gave up all pretense of being busy and considered the merits of passing out cold. There were quite a number of them, the first being that the topic of Gray Bennett would get dropped. That alone seemed worth the risk of banging herself on the head when she hit the beautiful rug. Besides, maybe the impact would knock some sense into her.

"I'm sorry, Joy. I can be a little too direct sometimes."

"I don't mind that." Joy brought her head up with care. "But I have to be honest with you. I don't feel comfortable talking about him."

"I totally understand." There was a pause and then Cassandra smiled. "May I at least ask what you're going to wear tonight?"

"Ah, I don't know. I don't really have anything fancy. I didn't expect to be going out."

"How'd you like to borrow something of mine?" Cass asked.

As Joy looked at the woman, she could have sworn the redhead had a twinkle in her eye.

GRAY STEPPED OUT OF the elevator and looked down Cassandra's hall.

His seminar had gone fine, but overall, he'd had a hellish day. Chasing down the gossip about Roger Adams's infidelity wasn't fun. And he'd hoped Beckin's source about the affair would be equivocal. The guy hadn't been. Apparently, the reporter, Anna Shaw, had come out of Adams's room, and when confronted with a witness, had run red-faced in the opposite direction. With her heels kicking up, the rear slit of her raincoat had flipped open to reveal a tiger-print Victoria's Secret number. And a whole lot of skin.

Now, again, one story didn't mean Senator Adams was the leak or that he was cheating on his wife, Allison. It just didn't look good.

And there was something about the whole situation that troubled Gray. He couldn't put his finger on it yet, but he'd learned long ago that when his instincts started to fire, he better dig until he found out why.

He rang Cassandra's bell.

The door opened.

And a whole new Joy Moorehouse was revealed.

Gray felt his eyes pop out of his head and tried to compose himself.

No luck. He could not dial down his stare reflex and only prayed his tongue hadn't rolled out of his mouth and onto his tie.

She was wearing a low-cut black dress, the creamy swells of her breasts revealed more than they were concealed. There was no way she was wearing a bra and the silk was so fine, laid so lightly on her skin, it would only take a fingertip to brush the neckline aside. He could see himself nuzzling her while he went to work on the dress's zipper, wherever the damn thing was.

He looked up. Her hair was brushed out straight and lying down her back. He wanted to touch it, bury his face in it.

He wanted her all over him.

Gray cleared his throat and quickly buttoned his double-breasted jacket. Hiding what was happening to his body seemed not only polite, but an act of self-preservation. Not that she didn't know how affected he was. The high color on her cheekbones told him he'd embarrassed her, ogling her like that.

Yeah, he'd once been smooth with the women. Truly.

"Are you ready to go?" he asked, praying the answer was yes.

Because the caveman in him was pointing out, with admirable if tragic logic, that since she'd answered the ring, it was likely that Cassandra and the maid were not home. Which meant if he were to come inside and the door were to be closed behind him, he and Joy would be all alone. With plenty of privacy. And quite a number of beds to choose from.

"Uh, yes, I'm ready," she said, lifting her chin. Her fingers fiddled with the dress's neckline as if she weren't quite comfortable with what she was wearing.

Well, that made two of them.

She picked up a little black bag off the hall table and walked past him. She was wearing some perfume that drove him nuts it was so sexy. And those heels. They were a mile high and made her ankles look so delicate he wanted to carry her down to the car.

Ah, hell, she could have had combat boots on and he'd still want to pick her up.

He shut the door and followed her to the elevator. When the doors opened, he reached out to touch the small of her back to guide her. He stopped himself.

No. No touching.

Not unless she was taking a fall because of those

skyscraper pumps. And then only to save her from hurting herself.

Because if he got his hands on her—

"Where are we going?" she asked.

Her voice, low, quiet, was like getting stroked. He punched the button for the lobby and refused to look at her, focusing instead on the little blinking numbers overhead.

"The Congress."

"What?"

"It's an old private club here in town."

"Oh. Do I look all right?"

Yeah, how to answer that one without using the words "sexy," "as" or "hell."

"You'll pass."

The elevator came to a stop and he held the gate open for her. When she stepped by him, it was all he could do not to yank her back inside, hit the emergency stop button and get up under that dress of hers.

As they walked through the lobby, he thought it was clearly pep-talk time.

So listen up, Bennett, he lectured himself. She's someone else's woman. And whereas that wouldn't matter to most of the ladies who could fill out a dress like that, it was still Joy Moorehouse inside the stunning, sexy creation.

So back the hell off.

MAYBE THE DRESS wasn't such a good idea, Joy thought as she got into the limousine.

You'll pass.

Now there was a ringing endorsement.

In fact, ever since Gray had given her a once-over

at the door, he'd fallen into a tense silence. She had to wonder if he knew she was just posing as a sophisticate. Maybe the lie annoyed him.

She really wished she could go back up and change into the black pants and sweater that were hers. However modest, at least she'd felt like herself in those clothes.

As the limousine took off down Park Avenue, Joy glanced across the leather seat. Gray was staring out the window, elbow on the door, chin on his fist. His eyebrows were down low, as if he were in the middle of an argument.

"You know, maybe this wasn't such a good idea," she blurted.

His head turned. "Are you tired?"

Ah, not likely. Starbucks had nothing on the nervous buzz she was riding.

"You just seem preoccupied," she said. "And I really don't have to go to dinner with you. I can go out on my own. In fact, why don't we just head our separate ways when we get—"

"Joy, no offense, but shut up."

Her eyes flared as he turned away.

Okay. Clearly she'd misread him. He wasn't silent because she'd irritated him, he was rip-roaring mad.

She studied his profile. Underneath that expensive black suit, behind the civilized guise of the flashy silk tie and gold cuff links, he was rigid with some kind of dark emotion. As if she'd offended him. Or said something that had pissed him off.

"I'm sorry," he muttered a minute later. "I'm a bastard when I get in this kind of mood."

"What's the matter? Did your meetings go badly?"

He laughed in a harsh burst. “Right now, I can’t even remember what I did all day.”

“Do you want to be alone?”

Gray’s eyes slid over to her face. His expression was so intense, she had to blink. It was either that or have her retinas toasted.

“No. I don’t want to be alone,” he said in a low, husky voice. His eyes flickered downward for a split second before he looked away. “And that’s my problem.”

Joy let her breath out slowly and glanced down at herself. In the dim glow of the interior lights, the curves of her chest were obvious. Lush. Even to her, her breasts looked swollen, inviting.

The limousine came to a stop and the door was opened by a man in a green-and-gold uniform. Gray got out first and then offered her a hand.

Joy thought back to what Cassandra had said, about the two of them not being lovers. The woman didn’t strike Joy as a liar. So if there was nothing going on between Gray and the beautiful widow, then what happened that night in his library just might have had nothing to do with the other woman. And everything to do with Joy.

And he’d wanted her when they’d danced together, hadn’t he?

An utterly reckless thought occurred to her. After a decade of dreaming, she was actually out in the big city with Gray. On what might be considered some form of date. And he’d noticed her.

It seemed as if she had a shot at making her pipe dream come true.

Gray leaned down and looked into the limousine. “You coming?”

One shot. And she was going to take it.

Joy reached out and slid her palm into his so their skin rubbed together. Gray's fingers twitched, as if he felt the same heat she did, and then he gripped her hand and pulled her up.

As she got out, she led with her upper body and turned so she was half facing him. She didn't have the nerve to meet him in the eyes, but she made sure she brushed her hip against his body as she stepped forward.

His sharp intake of breath gave her some confidence.

As they walked through a set of ornate doors, she sifted through every romantic movie she'd ever seen. She'd never tried to come on to a man before and she wished she was better prepared.

Seduction for Dummies. Now why hadn't someone written that bestseller?

"Bennett! How are you?" A man in his forties came up to them, eyeing Joy with admiration. "And who's this?"

"Joy Moorehouse, this is William Pierson IV," Gray said tersely before steering her away from the man.

In the time it took to get from the front door to their table at a window in the formal dining room, Gray must have talked to thirty people. He seemed to know everyone in the club and the delay gave her a little time to shore up her nerve.

She could do this. She really could. If Eve had pulled off the seducer routine with only an apple and some coaching from a snake, surely Joy could make a go of it in a Stella McCartney dress and a pair of Jimmy Choos.

But as Gray helped her with her chair and then sat down across from her, she hesitated. He didn't exactly look like a candidate for corruption. While he ordered a bourbon for himself and a glass of Chardonnay for her, his mood was grim. Maybe even worse than it had been in the limousine.

Had she read him wrong? She decided to do a little test. She pushed back her hair and then let her hand drift down the front of the dress. She paused, tugging at the neckline.

His eyes instantly snagged on what she was doing. And that dark moodiness lifted a little, revealing a pounding lust that just about blew her out of her chair.

Okaaay. Guess we're clear on that.

Wine. Wine would be good right now, she thought, taking a sip.

"So what did you do today?" she asked.

He looked up from the front of her dress. Leaned in toward her.

"Let me give you a piece of advice, Joy," he said. "You might want to think twice before trying to get my attention. I'm not a nice guy, someone who's going to take well to being teased."

She nearly dropped her glass as he picked up his bourbon and tossed the thing back.

Joy took a deep breath.

"What if I'm not teasing?" she said.

GRAY ALMOST CHOKED. He'd counted on her backing down.

But before he could say anything, a tuxedoed waiter appeared at their table. "Have you made your selections?"

Um, yeah, Gray thought. I'll have the total body

meltdown with a side of what-the-hell-was-I-thinking. She, evidently, will be having the sex-goddess potpie.

"We need a minute," he said. "But I'd like another bourbon."

The waiter nodded with deference and dematerialized.

Gray looked across the table, thinking now was his chance to be a gentleman. To prove that he still had a shred of decency left.

"Joy, you don't mean that. You're away from home, away from your real life. It's easy to be reckless."

"Are you saying that you're not..." She didn't finish.

"Attracted to you?"

She nodded.

"At this moment, I want you so badly my hands are shaking." Her eyes widened so he pressed harder, thinking maybe he could shock her into a retreat. "I want to take that dress off of you with my teeth, run my hands up and down your body, and then do the same thing with my mouth. How's that for attracted? And it gets worse. Every one of those men we just ran into? Each time they looked at you, I wanted to assault them."

The waiter came with the bourbon. Although Gray was tempted to hammer the damn thing, he made himself slow down. He needed to stay tight.

God, did he need to stay tight.

"But it's not right, Joy."

"Why not?"

"Because I don't want you to get hurt and because, quite frankly, I don't deserve you."

"Gray, that's not true—"

"Yeah, the hell it's not. I'm willing to bet sex means more to you than it does to me." He sipped his drink.

"I've left a lot of women the morning after and never looked back. It's not something I'm proud of, but I can't ignore what I've done, and I don't want to do that to you. I like you, Joy. I really do. And you're worthy of a lot more than a cold pillow."

That seemed to quiet her down.

And this time, when her hand went to the dress's neckline, she pulled the edges closer together.

"I wish I were a different kind of man," he said softly. "Because I would love to be with you. God, I'd really love to."

For the rest of the dinner, Joy put on a game face. They talked about her sister's wedding and Cassandra's dress and New York history, all the while picking at their food and fidgeting in their chairs. By the time they left, Gray could tell the strain was wearing on her.

Hell, it was wearing on him, too.

When the limousine pulled up in front of Cassandra's, he got out first.

"I'll take you up," he said.

"That's not necessary." As she stepped from the car, she smiled over her shoulder, the expression aimed somewhere to the left of him. "Thanks for dinner."

He walked into the lobby with her.

"Really, Gray, I can find my way."

"Humor me. It's a gentleman thing," he said, punching the elevator button. "My father and I live together. So he's still capable of grounding me."

They rode up in silence and he waited while she took out a key and opened the door. The penthouse was dark inside.

"Thanks again," she said, going in and feeling around for a light.

"Here, let me help you find the switch." He stepped forward into the apartment.

The door shut on its own behind him.

As he patted the wall, he leaned to the right just when she stepped to the left. Their bodies touched in the dark.

Gray froze. So did she.

The city's ambient glow was coming in through the windows across the room, and now that his eyes had adjusted, he could make out the lines of her face. The curves of her body.

Damn it, she was so close, he could smell her.

Get out of this apartment, he thought. Right now.

"Gray?" she whispered.

"What?" He was surprised he could get the word out. His jaw was so tight, he figured he'd need a crowbar to eat again.

"You're right about being away from home and feeling impulsive."

He let out his breath. Thank God, she saw things reasonably.

"And if we were anywhere near the lake, I would never ask you this." She looked up at him. "But will you kiss me? Just once? I've wanted to know what it would be like for…a while. No strings. Nothing weird. Just a kiss."

Gray's body slammed into overdrive.

"That's not a good idea," he said roughly.

She looked down. "I know. Forget I asked—"

"Because I don't know if I'll be able to stop."

Her face lifted.

"Oh, God, Joy." His voice didn't even sound like his

own. It was as thick as his blood had become. "You are so damned beautiful."

"I'm glad you like the dress."

"Screw the dress. It's got nothing to do with what you're wearing."

She reached out and put her hand on his lapel. "Kiss me. Once. Please."

That did it. He couldn't turn away. He just didn't have the willpower.

Gray moved in close, smoothing back her hair and then taking her face in his hands. Her lips parted and her eyes closed as he tilted back her head. He felt her body go completely still. She didn't seem to breathe at all. It was as if she had focused all her energy on what was about to come.

Frankly, he felt humbled.

Stroking her cheek with his thumb, he bent down, keeping his eyes on her face. He put his mouth softly on hers.

That was all he intended. Really.

Except the slight shudder that went through her was so erotic, he kissed her lightly again. Just a stroke of mouth on mouth with hardly any pressure at all behind the contact. Her hands crept up his chest and linked around his neck.

He brought his lips back down and this time he wasn't quite so gentle. In response, she leaned into him, her body coming against his. The fit of her fulfilled every idiotic cliché he'd ever heard. Lock and key. Hand and glove.

He wondered what taking her would feel like and imagined himself inside of her. Buried deep. Moving.

Dear God. The moving.

Gray heard a groan and realized it had come out of him. Before he could stop himself, he dug his hands into her hair and slipped his tongue into her mouth. She was so sweet, he almost hit the floor. A combination of the spearmint tea she'd had for dessert and something that was altogether her.

Her hands gripped his shoulders and he put his arms around her, bringing her hard against his body. Thigh to thigh, chest to breast, he absorbed the soft feel of her while backing her against the wall.

"I've got to go," he said over her mouth before kissing her again.

His hands skimmed her waist and hips and the dress was a flimsy barrier between him and her body. He could feel every bit of her as he slid his hands around her rib cage and paused under her breasts.

"Damn it…" he moaned against her lips. "We have to stop."

But he only kissed her harder, urgency getting the better of him. And instead of pulling away, she wrapped one leg behind his calf and rubbed him.

His control snapped.

JOY HAD ALWAYS IMAGINED it would be like this with Gray.

She was up against the wall, his hard body all over hers, his lips and tongue doing spectacular things to her mouth, his touch hot and a little rough. When his hand found her breast, she called out his name.

"Tell me to stop," he said hoarsely. *"Please."*

"Never."

With a groan of frustration, he gripped the leg she'd wrapped around his, bending it up to his hips and sinking his lower body into hers. She felt his arousal, thick and hot, and grabbed onto his backside, pulling him even closer. His hand shot underneath the dress's skirt, running up her thigh until he got to the garter belt she'd borrowed.

When his fingers reached the bare skin of her upper leg, he said something incoherent against her lips. And then his mouth was moving over hers again.

She was too inexperienced and overwhelmed to do anything more than hold on to him as he unleashed himself on her body. But he didn't seem to need anything more from her. No, he knew exactly what to do.

"Which bedroom are you in?" he asked.

"Down the hall. Second door. Left."

He scooped her up and started walking.

As he strode along, his face was familiar and strange at the same time. It was still the same bones, still the same dark hair framing the features, but arousal had transformed him. His eyes were dilated, almost unseeing. His brows were down tight. His skin was flushed and his breath was punching out of his mouth.

Looking at him, she thought about telling him she was a virgin, but the last thing she wanted was to give him an excuse to put a lid on their passion. It was her body. Her choice to have him. Besides, she was familiar enough with sex to know she was so turned on it wasn't going to hurt that badly. Maybe he wouldn't even know.

Gray kicked open the door to her room and carried her over to the queen-size bed. After he laid her down, he shut them in, throwing the lock.

There was no going back, she thought as she watched him come at her. He was going to stay and make love to her. And yes, he was probably going to leave and never look back. And yes, she would be devastated.

But she had him right now.

Looming over her, he tore off his jacket and tossed it onto a chair. Then he wrenched his tie from his neck.

Her body arched up for him as he joined her on the bed.

"Are you sure, Joy?" he asked. "Are you sure you want this?"

She nodded and buried her hands into his thick hair. "Oh, yes. I am very sure."

He closed his eyes for a moment.

And then he kissed her.

The dress melted away under his hands. He seemed to know precisely how to work the zipper and buttons and she tried not to think about how many women he must have undressed to be that fast.

Any such preoccupation flew from her mind as he looked at her body. He was positively reverent and he slowed down, touching her softly, stroking her neck and her collarbone and then moving downward.

He kissed her again, his tongue sliding into her mouth, and she felt his palm on her breast, the sensation jolting her back off the bed. When his lips sought out her nipple, she was utterly gone, incoherent, lost in him.

So she was only dimly aware that one of his hands had moved between her legs.

At least until he touched her heat.

"Gray!"

He lifted his head, his hooded eyes conflicted. "Am I going too fast?"

"I love you," she breathed.

"What?" His eyes peeled open with shock.

She winced. Oh, no. She couldn't possibly have let that out.

But when she looked up at him, she saw she wasn't the only one cringing. God, if he were any more horrified, they could have used his expression as a Halloween mask.

"Nothing. It was nothing," she said in a rush. Then she covered her face with her hands.

Oh, sure, she wasn't about to rush into the whole Virgin Speech. But she was more than willing to kill the moment with the only other thing that could hit a man like cold water.

I love you.

As Gray jumped off the bed, she grabbed the duvet and covered herself up. It seemed only fair considering he was making a beeline for his jacket and tie.

"Listen, I really need to go," he said back to her.

Yeah, I bet you do, she thought.

She wanted to tell him that she hadn't meant it, but nothing she could say now could change the effect of the words. Nothing was going to get them back to where they'd been.

And calling more attention to what had come out of her mouth was not going to help anyway. At this point, it would be like looking at a mushroom cloud on the horizon and saying, "Hey, you don't suppose a bomb just went off? Maybe we need to get moving here."

Besides, he really should leave. There were a couple of things she had to get to urgently. Like throwing up in the bathroom. Bursting into tears. That sort of thing.

He paused at the door. Looked back at her. "You are…"

Go ahead, she thought. Say it.

She was a total fool. She'd embarrassed them both. God, why had she let those words come out of her mouth?

"I'm sorry," she said.

He shook his head. "You're not the one who should be apologizing. I am. I should never have let things go so far."

"Let's just forget this ever happened, okay?"

"Yeah. Let's…do that."

The moment the door closed silently behind him, Joy shot off the bed and went for the shower. Under a blistering-hot spray, she scrubbed the makeup off her face and washed her skin as if in doing so she could go back to the start of the evening.

She paused with the bar of soap on her upper arm.

Or at least back to the part where Gray was on top of her, his eyes wild, his breathing labored, his big body straining to get into hers.

She closed her eyes. He had felt so good.

He'd been a taste of ecstasy.

Why did she have to go and make a mess out of everything? Hell, he probably thought she had stalker tendencies. Or was after his money.

And she'd proven she was about as sophisticated as a root vegetable.

One shot. And she'd blown it completely.

GRAY STALKED INTO his suite at the Waldorf.

She hadn't meant it. She couldn't possibly have meant it.

But then he thought of her eyes staring up at him before she'd realized what she'd said. They'd been glowing. She'd believed the words when they'd left her mouth.

Sweet girl. Beautiful, sweet Joy.

What a mess.

Although, man, he couldn't remember ever being so turned on. She'd been like warm honey under his mouth and hands, her skin softer than any he'd touched, her scent more delicious than any perfume. She'd made him feel male all the way down to his chromosomes. Hot. Hard. Powerful. Every time her breath had come out in a hiss or her body had surged under him, he'd wanted all of her. He'd wanted to take everything she was offering and then demand more. He'd wanted to consume her, burn her up from the inside and catch fire himself.

So thank God she'd spoken when she had. If she was naive enough to confuse great sex with emotions, she was absolutely the wrong woman for him.

Not that he'd ever doubted it.

But damn it, leaving her had been so hard. He'd hated the look of mortified embarrassment on her face as he'd bolted for the door. He'd wanted to tell her she had nothing to be ashamed of. That she was beautiful and he was running from her because he had to, because it was the right thing to do. Because she deserved to be treated with respect.

Except as he'd stood at the door, he'd been tongue-tied. And quite sure that if he stayed a moment longer, he just might have gone back to her.

At least they were driving up to Saranac Lake together tomorrow. In the daylight, he'd tell her everything he hadn't been able to tonight. He'd make it right between them.

As Gray took off his clothes, he caught a whiff of her

perfume on his shirt. The scent hardened him again and brought back the kind of images he knew damn well were going to keep him up all night long.

For the next month. Or two. Or six.

He got into bed, turned off the light and stared into the darkness.

Five hours of tossing and turning later, dawn came and he watched the sun come up, wishing Joy was with him. When room service brought him the breakfast he'd ordered, he wondered idly if she would have shared what was on his plate. Did she take her eggs scrambled? Over easy? He would have enjoyed feeding her bits of croissant, and if she liked strawberry jam, even better. He could have licked the sweetness from her lips.

Maybe she would have licked it from his fingers.

He went to his meeting aching as though his skin had shrunk or his body had swelled. And when he pulled up in front of Cassandra's building, he couldn't help imagining what would have happened if he'd stayed. He and Joy would have made love two or three times during the night. He'd have satisfied her until she was hoarse from calling out his name and then he'd have had the pleasure of watching her sleep in his arms.

It was hard not to feel as if he'd cheated them both.

But it was better to have walked away when he did. Hell, his retreat was arguably moral, a righteous act of self-control he could use to balance the scales against all the crap he pulled for a living.

"Mr. Bennett?" The doorman's voice was muffled as Rodney peered through the car window. "Are you waiting for someone?"

Yeah, wrong verb there, buddy. Try *desperate.*

Gray got out. "I'm picking up Mrs. Cutler's guest. I'll be right back."

The doorman tipped his hat as Gray strode into the lobby. Cassandra was just coming out of the elevators.

She looked a little confused as she saw him. "Did she forget something?"

"Sorry?"

"Joy. Did she leave something behind?"

He frowned. "I'm here to pick her up."

"She's already left. She took a train back early this morning. Didn't she tell you?"

Gray felt a strange kind of panic. "No, she didn't."

Cass's eyes narrowed. "That's odd."

He dragged a hand through his hair and cursed, thinking if he drove like a bat out of hell, he could be at White Caps in four hours.

"Did she, uh, did she look okay?"

"Maybe a little tired. She said she couldn't wait to get home, but other than that, she was perfectly happy."

Perfectly happy.

And then it hit him. She was on her way back to Tom.

Tom. Her boyfriend.

"Gray, are you all right?"

He smiled, thinking his cheeks were going to split open. "I'm great."

"Sure you are. You look miserable. What's wrong?"

"Talk to you later, Cass."

Gray went back to his car. By the time he was on the New York Thruway heading north, he decided it was best not to make White Caps his first stop when he got to the Adirondacks.

Best not to make it any destination at all.

Though he would never forget those moments between them, she was, after all, going home to her boyfriend. And in the light of day, she was no doubt relieved that things hadn't gone any further.

A narrow escape, he thought. They'd both had a narrow escape.

Because a small voice in the back of his pea brain told him that once he'd had her, he'd want her again.

CHAPTER SEVEN

THREE WEEKS, GRAY THOUGHT. Three damn weeks and I still can't get that woman out of my head.

He eyed the squash ball coming at him as if it were alive and carrying a knife. Slamming the face of his racket into the thing, he sent it into the wall with vicious force. The ball ricocheted wildly out of bounds and almost caught his partner in the chest on the rebound.

Sean O'Banyon, a powerhouse on Wall Street, and no momma's boy even on Mother's Day, came at Gray like a tank.

"Goddamn it! That's four times I've had to duck for cover!"

As the guy pulled up just short of their chests touching, it was easy to see the South Boston street thug Sean used to be. If Gray wanted a fight instead of the civilized game they were supposed to be playing, he was going to get one from his friend. Right here. On the squash courts of the elite Congress Club.

No wonder folks called Sean "SOB." And not just because of the man's initials.

"What the *hell* is your problem, Bennett?"

Yeah, where to start with that.

Gray cursed. "Sorry. I'm trying to burn my edge off. It's not working."

And he should have known a quick game of squash

wouldn't help much. Chasing a little ball around wasn't going to bust through the frustration of three weeks of insomnia, three weeks of being tortured by hot dreams, three weeks of missing a woman he wasn't supposed to be missing.

What he needed was Joy.

On top of him. In his arms.

And now that he was back in New York? Naturally, she was on his mind every second of the day.

God, only poll results used to get him this preoccupied.

Sean stepped back. Bounced a ball on his racket. "You got problems?"

Gray shook his head. "I'm just on a hair trigger right now. I should have warned you."

"Or we should have gotten in a ring together." Sean smiled darkly. "Listen, why don't we shower and head to the bar? You look like you could use a drink and I have no interest in needing a cardiac surgeon."

"Can't. I'm due at Allison and Roger Adams's in an hour. They're throwing a party for Ken Wright."

Sean cocked an eyebrow as they walked over to the court's exit. "Wright's running for mayor, isn't he?"

Gray held the door open for his friend. "Yeah, but his campaign's in the crapper. He's hired me as a hail Mary, last-minute miracle, so from now until November, you'll have plenty of opportunities to get me back. I'm going to be mostly here in Manhattan for the duration."

"I'm always up for a game." Sean laughed coldly. "Or a fight."

"And you think I've got issues?"

"At least I kept my balls in fair territory today."

Gray smiled as they walked down the marble corridor, nodding to other members who were also dressed in whites. The men's locker room was down on the left, marked by a pair of glossy black doors. Inside, the air was heavy with steam and the mingling of different aftershaves. Mahogany lockers with brass nameplates ran from floor to ceiling behind a fleet of varnished benches.

They stripped and went into the old-fashioned, communal shower. The twenty-by-twenty-foot room was white-tiled on all sides with four drains set into the floor and at least a dozen showerheads on the walls. They took two in the back.

"So what's her name?" Sean asked as they cranked the chrome fixtures.

The rush of water drowned out Gray's curse.

"You want to try that again?" Sean prompted dryly.

"There's no her."

"Yeah, right." Sean worked a bar of soap in his hands and then covered his face with suds. "Come on, Bennett. Talk to me."

To buy some time, Gray squeezed some shampoo into his hand and then rubbed the stuff through his hair. "I've lost my mind, SOB. I really have."

Sean made a noncommittal noise through spray. "On account of?"

"Her name's Joy."

Rich, masculine laughter made Gray wish he'd clammed up.

"Nice name, Bennett. This someone you're sleeping with or working on?"

"I'm not sleeping with her." Gray realized he was

blushing and stuck his head under the water. "I'm just desperate to."

"So take her to bed. What's the problem?"

"It's complicated."

Because after replaying everything that had happened between them over and over again, he just didn't know whether Joy was the sweet, gentle girl he'd always assumed her to be, or a calculating woman capable of giving even him a run at the sex game. Every time he thought about how amazing she'd been with him, how high she'd taken them both, he reminded himself that she'd been with him while that poor Opie guy was waiting for her back home.

"And the problem is?" Sean prompted, squeezing shampoo onto his palm.

"I respect who I've always thought she was too much to be with her. And I can't bear who she might be."

"Yeah, that makes sense."

"It does. One of the most attractive things about her was her…God, I guess you'd call it innocence. I've known her for years, since she was a teenager. I was so sure she wasn't…"

"Like the others?" SOB arched under the spray to rinse his hair out.

"Yeah. I was feeling guilty as hell for wanting her like I did and that was even before I saw her with her boyfriend. Then she came here to the city, we hooked up and it was insanely hot…" Gray soaped his chest. "But, damn, she's with someone and she let me crawl all over her. What kind of decent woman pulls that stuff?"

It was his mother's favorite game and look where that had landed them all.

"How'd you leave it with her?" Sean asked.

In the middle, Gray thought. And he'd been a sexually frustrated madman ever since.

"I left when she told me she loved me."

Sean dropped the bar of soap he was using on his legs. "What?"

"It wasn't like that. She didn't mean it. She couldn't possibly have. But it shocked enough sense into me to get me out the door."

"Yeah, those three little words will bring a man back to reality, all right."

"I just can't figure out who she is. If she's the nice girl I've always assumed she is, I can't be with her because I'll do one hell of a number on her."

"But what if she's not?"

"Well, I guess that's a different story. Except I don't know if I want the truth." The letdown would be oddly painful.

With a final rinse, Sean turned his water off. "She in town?"

Gray shut down his showerhead. "No. Up north."

Water dripped onto the tile with a casual, tinkling sound. After grabbing thick white towels from a neat pile in the corner, they went back to the lockers.

"The thing is, I can't stop thinking about her." Gray opened his and took out his shirt, shrugging into the button-down. "And the dreams. Holy hell, I feel like I'm fourteen. I wake up every morning with a—well, you know what I mean."

"If memory serves, yeah." Sean's dark smile returned as he hit his pits with some deodorant spray. He tossed the can over so Gray could use it. "You got it bad, my boy. You got it real bad."

After pulling on his boxers, Gray stepped into his

pin-striped slacks and tucked the shirt in with vicious stabs of his hand. "Maybe I just need to get busy with another woman."

But as soon as he said the words, the idea didn't appeal.

"Don't know if substitution's really going to work in this case," SOB drawled, pulling a black cashmere sweater over his head. "Sounds like you're not hard up for sex. You're hard up for her."

Gray shot his buddy a glare, even though he knew the guy was absolutely right. "You're not giving me a whole lot of relief here."

"You want a kiss-ass liar, talk to someone else." Sean strapped on a heavy gold watch. "My advice? Get her out of your system. Ask the woman to come down for a visit, hole up in your suite with her and don't leave until the mystery's gone. What you have is a classic case of obsession. A little exposure therapy and you'll be back to normal in no time. Unless of course…"

Sean brushed his black hair straight back from his proud forehead.

"What?" Gray paused in the middle of knotting his tie. *"What?"*

"Unless she's the real deal for you. In which case you're screwed." Gray started cursing and Sean laughed. "But the probability of that is next to zero. Men like you and me, we're not hardwired for that kind of thing."

Gray thought about it for a moment. "You might be right. But she's with someone."

"That's between her and him. It's got nothing to do with you."

"Man, you're tough."

"You're only figuring that out now?"

After they left the locker room, Sean headed for the bar while Gray strode out into the lobby. He wasn't in a big hurry to get to Allison and Roger's party. Just this morning, he'd finally tracked down the last source Beckin had given him about Roger's nocturnal exploits with that reporter. The story had been corroborated again.

It was time to have a sit-down with Adams about what had happened. Gray was hoping there was some kind of logical explanation other than that of the horizontal variety, although what it might be, he hadn't a clue. And if the situation was indeed as bad as it looked, he was in a hell of a spot if the man hadn't told his wife. Allison had every right to know, but she really should hear it from her husband.

God, of all the marriages he'd ever known, theirs had seemed the most solid.

Gray was striding across the dark marble of the Congress Club's lobby, heading for the door, when the hair on the back of his neck came to attention. He glanced around. There were a number of people in the place, but none who'd make his instincts come to attention—

"Gray."

The smooth sound of his mother's voice made him shut his eyes for a moment before he turned around.

Goddamn, Belinda was still beautiful. Dark hair, just like his, thick, loose and glowing on her shoulders. Hazel eyes tilted at the corners. Expertly made-up and surgically maintained face. Naturally, she was dressed to kill in clothes only big money could afford. And just as expected, there was some man by her side. The guy was an older version of the type she'd always gone for. Handsome, well-dressed, vacant-eyed and polite.

"Hello, *Mother*. Who's your friend?"

"This is Stuart. Stuart, my son Gray."

Gray nodded and let the guy's hand hang in the breeze. "Nice to meet you, Stu. Now if you two love birds will excuse me, I was just leaving."

"Grayson, a moment, please." His mother's eyes flashed and she stepped forward. As if she were prepared to follow him out of the club.

"Aren't you busy?" Gray drawled, flipping Stu a glance.

Belinda leaned back and ran a hand down the man's cheek, as if she were stroking something she owned. "Stuart, excuse us, darling, won't you?"

Stuart smiled at her, kissed her mouth and left.

Bet he fetches slippers and the paper real well, too, Gray thought as his mother cleared her throat with a little cough.

"Your father," she said quietly. "How is he?"

"Why the hell would you care?"

"He's been ill. Of course I want to know how he is."

"Well, you can get the update from someone else." Gray started walking away, hoping to get free of her. On the rare occasions their paths crossed, she always wanted to talk about the past, as if he were some kind of confessor.

But going through his childhood once was enough.

When he heard the sound of high heels clicking softly on the marble behind him, he knew he wasn't going to get away with a quick-and-easy parting.

"Grayson!" she hissed.

He stopped, glared over his shoulder and then stepped into an alcove. "What."

She took a moment to collect herself. "You know, Gray, just because your father and I weren't...compatible, doesn't mean you have to hate me."

Gray jammed his hands into his pockets. Though he was bored to death with the predictable subject, somehow he never failed to rise to the bait when pressed. And if she wanted to try for a shot at redemption from him, then she was going to pay for the privilege by being a target for his anger.

"Interesting how you reduce it all to compatibility," he muttered.

"Your father and I were never well-suited."

"Yeah, you two had some real irreconcilable differences, didn't you? Starting with the fact that you are a whore and he was looking for a wife."

She stiffened regally. "I don't appreciate being addressed in such a crude manner."

"Then stop chasing after me." Gray's hand went to the knot of his tie. Beneath the silk, his throat was tight.

"You're just as bad as your father. Completely intractable. There's no reasoning with either one of you."

"And there's no way to keep you off your back, is there?"

She paled. "Grayson! I'm your mother!"

"I know," he said dully, stomach churning. "Believe me, I know."

He looked around the lobby. There weren't many people around and he knew their hushed voices weren't carrying far, but he'd be damned if he was going to have it out with her in public.

"Anyway, sorry, I can't chat," he lied. "I'm late for an engagement."

She didn't even seem to hear him. "You shouldn't judge other people's relationships."

"You're my parents. I had to live with the fallout of what you did to my father. So I'm damn qualified to judge."

"He never loved me."

"That's where you're wrong."

"He loved his books and the law and his work. I was nineteen when we married, twenty when I had you. He was twelve years older than I was, ensconced in his career. He left us both alone up at the lake for months while he was in D.C."

"You were *never* alone."

Memories of her against the side of the house at the lake, a man's hands under her dress, her head back and eyes closed, hit Gray like a pile driver. He'd been thirteen when he'd caught that little show. The echoes of her laughter, so high, shrill and desperate, had woken him up for months afterward.

And he hadn't been alone, either. Shame had been his constant companion when he was a teenager. Knowing what his mother was up to. Keeping her secrets. Lying when his father called and she was out screwing some random guy.

Belinda opened her mouth, but he silenced her with his hand. "You know something? I'm no more interested in this conversation than I was the last ten times you cornered me somewhere. Goodbye, Mother, dear."

"I think of you, Grayson," she said starkly, grabbing his arm.

He flipped out of her grip and turned away. "And I think of you. All the damned time."

Gray burst through the ornate doors and cut through the rush of pedestrians on the sidewalk. As his limousine slid up and he got in, he became aware that his hands were in fists.

While the car sped down Park Avenue, he stared out the window, trying to collect himself and failing. When the driver pulled up to Allison and Roger's building, Gray couldn't make himself open the car door. For reasons he despised, his mother still had the capacity to make him feel like a lost boy instead of the man he was. The vulnerability pissed him off, and with his emotions bouncing around, he knew he wasn't fit for the social scene bubbling in the penthouse far above.

"You want to be taken somewhere else?" the driver asked when Gray didn't get out right away.

"No. Thanks."

Gray left the limousine and walked around the block a few times, the cold breeze seeping in through the worsted wool of his suit. When he was ready, he went through the building's lobby, got into the elevator and convinced himself he was sufficiently on autopilot so he could make it through what was left of the party.

Except the moment he put his foot through the Adams's door, he knew he was lying to himself. There were about a hundred people milling around the perfectly appointed penthouse, and though he knew all of them, they suddenly seemed like total strangers to him. Or maybe he just wished they were. The sound of people talking and laughing, the smell of hors d'oeuvres, the simmering, polite aggression as folks tried to one-up each other, it all hit him like an assault.

He turned to go back out the door.

"Gray!" Cassandra walked up and kissed his cheek. "I called you. Joy's here—"

His breath stopped. "In town?"

"Yes. At this party as a matter of fact. She—"

"Where is she?"

His eyes scanned the crowd, looking for strawberry-blond hair. His heart was in his throat, and though he felt pathetic about the desperation, he wanted to see her. Especially tonight.

"Maybe she's in the library," Cassandra murmured, glancing around with him. "I think she wanted to look at the books."

Gray knew the apartment's layout and moved through the guests as quickly as he could without being rude. He was about to go down a hallway when Roger Adams stepped in front of him.

"We were worried you weren't coming!" The senator was all smiles. "Did you catch Wright? He's over there, by the bar."

Gray stared down at the man he thought he'd known so well.

Fury, spurred by the chummy visit with his mother, sharpened his voice so it cut through the chatter. "We need to talk."

Adams's eyes narrowed. "What's wrong?"

At that moment, Allison, who was laughing with someone no more than four feet away, caught Gray's eye and blew him a kiss.

Adams reached out a hand. "Bennett, you look like hell. Come on, let's go to my study."

"No." Gray shook off the hold. "We're not going to do this tonight. And not here."

"Okay," Adams said slowly. "I'll be in Washington as of tomorrow. Is everything all right?"

"I'll see you down there at your office."

"Gray, what's going on?"

"Anna Shaw. That's what. And I'm not talking about the leaks."

"Oh…God." The senator's face paled first and then ran red. Sweat broke out over the man's upper lip. "Look, I—"

"No, save it. We'll do this in private. Not a yard away from your *wife*."

Gray turned away in disgust and stalked off. The last thing he wanted was for Allison to overhear anything. And besides, adultery was a subject he couldn't handle talking about tonight.

As he headed for the far corner of the penthouse, several people jumped in his path, but he shrugged them off harshly. He didn't have anything polite left in him. Thinking about the betrayal in the Adams's marriage made his own past come close enough to choke him. As if looking into his mother's face hadn't been bad enough.

He had some dim notion he should probably leave, but he wanted to see Joy. He just needed to…

Hell, if he was better at dealing with his emotions, he might have actually known what he needed from her. As it was, he just had an undeniable urge to be in the same room with Joy. To look into her eyes. To breathe the same air she did.

When he rounded the corner and saw the library's half-open door, he braced himself. What if she didn't want to see him? What if—

He looked inside.

There she was, facing the shelves, her head tilted up as she stroked the leather spine of a book. The black knit dress she wore was a second skin. Her hair spilled down her back. Her feet were in another pair of strappy numbers that made him want to kiss her arches.

Still hovering in the doorway, Gray scanned the room, half expecting there to be a man with her. But she was alone, as if she'd sought sanctuary from noisy strangers, and with the classical music swirling in the air, the party was nearly drowned out.

God, he wanted to shut them in together. Hold her. Find some peace. Give some to her.

He stepped forward only to feel someone brush past him.

"Bennett, how are you?" Charles Wilshire, one of New York's top tax attorneys, spoke quietly and held up two wineglasses. "I'd shake, but I'm taking care of a lady."

Gray's eyes narrowed as Wilshire walked over to Joy. She turned, keeping her back to the door, and took the glass he offered. Their hands touched.

CHAPTER EIGHT

"So you were about to tell me how long you've known Cassandra?"

Joy sipped her wine. The man standing in front of her was super-sophisticated in his navy-blue suit and he fit in with the rest of the people at the party. All the guests had the shiny freshness of big wealth, that ambient glow of disposable cash radiating from their clothes, their jewelry, their eyes. The whole lot of them just sparkled.

"I haven't known Cass long," she answered. "I designed a gown for her."

His eyes flared. "Really. What house are you with?"

"I'm on my own."

He glanced at her left hand. "And you came with Cassandra, too, didn't you? Not a husband."

She nodded. "I'm staying with her while I'm in town."

The man's eyes traced over her face.

When she'd walked into the party, he'd taken one look at her and cut a path through the crowd. His name was Charles something.

She'd been surprised because she was out of her league in borrowed clothes, although Charles Whoever apparently hadn't picked up on the subterfuge. As he didn't look like a stupid man, she had to assume she was a better actress than she'd thought.

"How long are you in town?" Charles asked. His smile was direct. So were his eyes. Neither were lewd.

"A couple of days. I'm doing the alterations here."

His gaze dipped lower. The dress's high neckline meant she wasn't showing a lot of skin, but the black knit fabric clung to her body. Just like his eyes did.

She glanced back to the orderly rows of books, wishing her thoughts could be so well cataloged and controlled. Being stared at by a man like that reminded her of Gray. When Gray had looked at her that way, she'd come apart in her own skin. Charles Whoever had no such effect on her.

Gray.

A familiar, achy sting nailed her in the chest. The emotion, a not-so-charming combination of shame, regret and impotent longing, evidently had the shelf life of a Twinkies. Because the damn feeling was as fresh as the moment when he'd left her mostly naked on that bed.

She took another sip of wine.

"Are you free for dinner tomorrow night?"

Joy looked over at the man in front of her, feeling flustered. He was very attractive in that slick, New York kind of way and not joking in the slightest. But she just wasn't attracted to him.

"I, uh—"

"God, you blush," he said in wonderment. As if the women he knew did nothing of the sort.

Charles Whoever reached out and brushed a lock of hair over her shoulder. His fingers lingered on the waves and she suddenly became aware that they were in a room that was very empty.

Time to get out of here, she thought.

But before she could make an excuse to leave, a deep voice cut through the classical music. “Hello, *Joy*.”

She spun around. Gray was standing behind her, big as one of Saranac’s mountains, dark as a summer thunderstorm. The cold control in his face suggested he was flat-out angry.

She nearly dropped her wineglass.

After three weeks of thinking about the man, seeing him in the flesh was like cozying up to a stun gun. On numb reflex, she absorbed his pin-striped suit, his bright red tie, his ultra-white shirt. She thought about how silky his thick hair had felt on her skin. How he had touched her with his hands. His mouth.

Her body responded in a blood rush, as if it recognized him as its own.

“And maybe we can shake now,” Gray drawled, offering his hand to Whoever. “Your wife here tonight, or are you flying solo?”

Whoever flushed. “No, uh, she’s gone down with the staff to open the Palm Beach house.”

Gray swirled a squat drink in his hand. Ice tinkled. “Imagine that. And the kids? How are they? Must be three and six now, right?”

“Um, yes. How good of you to remember.”

There was a tight silence.

Whoever looked out to the party. As though he couldn’t wait to get back to it.

“If you’ll excuse me,” he murmured to Joy. “It was a pleasure meeting you.”

"Yeah, run along, Charles," Gray bit out. "There's a good boy."

Joy watched Whoever go, trying to collect herself. When she looked up, Gray was staring at her, a hard line to his jaw. His brows. His shoulders.

All she could think of was, Thank God she hadn't called him.

She'd been tempted to. Desperate to take back her untimely confession, she'd often considered picking up the phone. She hadn't been sure what she would say, but the urge to try to delete, erase, do-over, was a powerful one. Now, though, she was proud of herself for walking away clean, for not embarrassing herself even more.

"Well, Joy, aren't you getting around," Gray said, finishing his drink. "And you seem so disappointed Charles has left. Or maybe you're just surprised that he's married? No, wait. I don't think that would bother you."

"What are you doing here?" she asked, because she couldn't think of anything else to say. His anger didn't make sense. His words didn't make sense.

"What are *you* doing here?"

Joy's spine tightened. "Cassandra invited me to come along with her."

"Quite the hostess that woman is."

A waiter walked in with another squat glass. Gray traded it for the one he'd emptied. "I want another. Now, not later."

The other man quickly disappeared.

As Gray downed the fresh bourbon or Scotch or whatever it was in two swallows, Joy thought she should probably follow the waiter's example. No one stayed in the path of an eighteen-wheeler, not if they had an ounce of common sense. And Gray was carrying one hell of a load of something tonight.

"If you'll excuse me—"

Gray's hand shot out and took her arm. "No, I don't think I will."

With one tug, he brought her close to his body. Heat rolled off of him, seething emotions and the promise of raw sex combined.

"You look good in that dress, Joy. But then I'm sure Charles said the same thing." Gray's voice was silky now, but that was just cover. His fingers were a vise. "And I'm surprised Wilshire ran off so fast. Then again, he frightens easy."

"Yeah, well, you'd intimate a lot of armed felons right now," she shot back.

As they glared at each other, Joy wondered why she wasn't more afraid. She remembered what Tom had said about Gray, that underneath the man's urbane window dressing, there was something scary hard about him. Except even though Tom was right, she knew Gray would never hurt her. He was chewed up inside about something, but he wouldn't physically harm her.

And sure enough, Gray's grip loosened and his thumb moved, caressing the inside of her wrist. Her breath quickened as his eyes became hooded.

"Tell me something, Joy. How is it possible that I've read you wrong after all these years?"

"Have you?"

"Oh, yes. Most definitely." He smiled in a way that made his teeth seem sharp. "So how's Tom?"

"I beg your pardon?"

"What's he doing right now, Joy? While you're here in that dress, letting some married man feel you up?

Is he sitting by the phone, waiting for you to call? Or did you tell him you were going to be really busy and would phone in the morning?"

"I don't know what he's doing," she said slowly and clearly. "Because I'm not with him."

"Not tonight you aren't."

"Ever."

"God, you're good. I think it's those wide eyes. You could convince a man hell was heaven, couldn't you?"

The waiter came back with yet another glass and Gray let go of her to do the exchange. The guy with the tray left in a hurry.

When Gray went to drink, she put her hand on his forearm. "I don't understand all this. Why are you so angry? What's the problem?"

His eyes narrowed. "You. You're the problem."

Ouch.

"Well, that's easily fixed. Goodbye, Gray." She turned away.

"I want you," he said baldly. "And it hurts."

Joy looked over her shoulder, wondering if she'd caught that right. "What?"

"You heard me."

He put the drink aside and moved in behind her so his chest was up against her back. He put his lips down next to her ear.

"I want you so much that right now, there's only one thing I need more than you." She felt his fingertip on her nape. It traveled slowly down her spine, the thin knit of the dress acting like a conductor for his touch. "I want you out of me. Out of my brain. Out of my body."

She expelled her breath as he continued, his voice husky. Deep.

"I can't forget what you felt like and I want to finish what we started. I shouldn't have left when I did, but I thought things were different then. If I'd known otherwise, I never would have stopped." His fingertip disappeared and was replaced by his knuckles. They rubbed the small of her back. "I *never* would have stopped."

In a flash of movement he spun her around and tucked her into his hips. His body was wild for her. She could feel every hard inch of his arousal.

"Tell me the truth," he demanded, eyes drilling into her. "Have you thought of me since that night?"

Of course she had, but she'd been so sure she'd killed his desire for her. Catching up to where he actually was, to his undiminished attraction to her, was one hell of a long road.

When she didn't speak, he stroked her neck. "Tell me, Joy. At night, when you're laying in your bed, do you ache for my mouth? Do you wish my skin was against yours? Do you imagine what it would be like to have me inside of you? *Answer me.*"

A smart woman would lie right now, she thought. Or keep her mouth shut.

"Yes." The word escaped from her lips.

He laughed with dark satisfaction. "Good. Because whenever I close my eyes, all I see is you on that bed. I remember what you tasted like. How you arched up off the mattress for me. I hear the way your breath broke when I had my mouth on your breast and my hand between your thighs."

She swayed toward him. She'd remembered the same things. She'd ached from wanting the very same things.

After three weeks of berating herself as an idiot, and being convinced he was never going to have anything to do with her again, the idea that he was as tortured and hungry as she was a hazardous relief.

"I thought I'd scared you off."

"And I was convinced I'd be doing you a disservice if I hunted you down. I've wanted to call you, see you, be with you, since the moment I left. Now I'm sorry I didn't come after you."

"I wish you had," she blurted.

"As do I… So let's leave. Right now. Let's go to my place." He slid his hand down to her hip. He squeezed and then caressed the curve of bone. "I'll make it good for you, Joy. Like no one else ever has. Or will."

God, she didn't doubt that for a second. But what about afterward?

When she stayed silent, he cupped her chin. "I promise you, I won't stop this time. No matter what you say or what you do." He bent his head and kissed her neck. Sucked her skin gently. "Come with me. Let's finish what we started."

As Joy stepped through the doorway of his suite, Gray was surprised by how hesitant she was. Her eyes avoided his, as though she were nervous, and she moved slowly, as if she were on unfamiliar, uneven ground.

Shutting the door and locking it, he reminded himself that she was the kind of woman who could string along a number of men. Tom, the miserable hometown honey she was walking all over. Charles, the lecherous bastard.

Gray, himself, the desperate son of a bitch who wanted her so badly he didn't care she was loose. Didn't care that she wasn't who he'd thought she was.

He watched her drift around the main room, her

hands running over varnished woods and satin draperies.

Damn it, that dress was making him woozy.

"So, uh…" She paused. Dropped her purse down on the silk couch. "I've never done this before."

That blush was back. The one that never failed to ensnare him. The one that had clearly worked its magic on Tom and Charles.

"Done what?" he asked dryly.

"Er—gone to a hotel room with a man."

The lie hardened Gray's heart, but had no effect whatsoever on his body.

Enough with the talking, he thought. He wanted her and the time had come.

Walking over to her, he tore off his jacket and worked his tie free in a series of jerks.

She held her hand out. "Wait."

"Why?" He stopped a mere foot away from her and kicked off his black wingtips. Tossed the tie aside.

She licked her lips, making his knees weak. "First I want an apology."

"You've got it." Anything to keep her with him tonight. He didn't care what it took.

"It's about Charles," she said, stepping back.

Oh, yeah, he *really* wanted to talk about another guy right now. "What about him?"

"Just because I'm standing next to some man, doesn't mean I'm…sleeping with him. I want you to apologize for jumping to that kind of conclusion."

"Fine. I'm sorry."

"You could say it like you mean it."

"I'm *very* sorry."

She shook her head. Crossing her arms, she hugged herself. “Maybe this was a mistake.”

“The hell it is. We need this.”

Gray yanked his shirt free from his waistband and started unbuttoning the thing. Her eyes darted to his throat as it was revealed and then followed down his bare chest. When he pulled the halves apart, her gaze drifted to his stomach.

Having her look at his naked skin made his erection throb against his fly like it was searching for the exit. But she was standing there in a kind of shock, as though he were about to jump her.

Absently he became aware of an ache in his chest.

He took a deep breath. Dragged a hand through his hair.

“Look, Joy, you’re free to leave, but you need to head for the door right now. I’m about to kiss you and once I do that, there’s no going back. Do you understand? Unless you’re prepared to wake up next to me in the morning, you better get out of here.”

He waited for her to decide. In the silence, his body hammered at his will, demanding to be set loose and take her. His eyes latched on to her lips. He could already feel them under his mouth as he kissed her long and deep.

“I’ll even go slowly,” he murmured, “after the first time. But you’ve got to make your mind up now. You’re killing me. Leave or let me inside.”

Her arms moved and he thought she was going for her purse.

Instead, she reached around to her side. He heard a zipper.

And then the dress hit the floor.

As Joy kicked the black fabric away with the toe of a high-heeled shoe, she fought the urge to shield herself with her hands. The embarrassment was a little absurd considering the matching black bra and panties showed no more than a bikini would. But then again, when she was in her bathing suit, she wasn't acutely aware that she was going to be naked in another minute and a half. Naked and with a man. With Gray.

Staring down at the rug, she waited for him to touch her. When he didn't move, she nearly cursed. Was there something wrong with her?

She lifted her hands to cover herself.

"No, please, no." His voice cracked. "Don't hide from me. I just want to look at you a little."

Her eyes flew up to his. His expression was reverent. His body super-still.

"I want…" he said. "I want to remember this."

When she dropped her hands, he reached out, stroking her hair back from her face and down over her shoulders. His body was throwing off serious arousal signals, but when he put his lips against hers, the contact was light. Soft. He kissed her over and over again until she relaxed completely and leaned into him.

The sensation of his bare torso against her breasts and belly was luscious.

"Will you touch me?" he moaned, taking her hands and putting them on his chest. "Please…just touch me."

Her palms flattened over his pecs. Under a dusting of dark hair, his skin was hot, a smooth layer of satin over hard contours. His heart was pumping fast, as if he were running.

While his tongue gently penetrated her mouth, she ran her hands over male muscles that were tight, straining. She felt his body shudder and jerk as she went south, across the ridges of his abdomen. His bucking response was exactly what she needed to feel, a great equalizer. He may have been the experienced one, but his desperation put her in the driver's seat. She slid her arms around him and ran her hands up his back, under the shirt.

"Bed," he groaned, grabbing her backside and pulling her against him, his arousal pressing into her belly. "Need a bed. *Now.*"

He maneuvered them around various pieces of furniture, his mouth doing crazy things to hers while they stumbled into a darkened room. She felt something come up against the back of her calves and then he was reaching down, whipping some kind of comforter back. A shift in his weight had her falling to the mattress and he followed, one of his knees parting her thighs. He drove his hips against hers, his hard length hitting just the right spot.

Her nails dug into him as she bowed off the bed and he took advantage of her arch, unclasping her bra and sweeping it from her body. His mouth found her breast and the sweet sucking distracted her as he slid her panties off. When he pulled back, she looked down between their bodies. In the dim glow coming from the lights in the living room, she saw he was working his belt with quick hands. And then his pants and his boxers were gone.

He still had the shirt on, but the whole front of him was bare as he lay down on top of her. The feel of all his skin against hers made her eyes roll back in her head. And then he was burying his lips in her throat, his body moving sinuously against hers in a surging rhythm, his arousal a hot brand on the inside of her thigh. She didn't want to wait any longer. Couldn't. She'd lived with the frustration of wanting for too long.

"Gray, I need…"

"Yeah, I know," he growled thickly. "Me, too."

His weight shifted and she grabbed on to him, trying to bring him back to the cradle of her hips. Dimly, she heard a drawer being opened, but she paid little attention. She was too busy wrapping her legs around his to hold him in place.

"Easy, beautiful." His voice was so hoarse she could barely understand the words. "I'm getting ready as quick as I can."

He lifted himself off of her and when he settled between her thighs again, his breath was ragged. The muscles of his body were quivering and twitching as he reached down and touched her most sensitive skin. She arched up against him, crying out.

"Oh, woman." His head dropped to her shoulder. "You want this as badly as I do."

His weight shifted. His fingers disappeared.

"Hold on to me," he said into her ear. "This is going to be fast and hard, but I'll make it up to you."

And then he entered her in a powerful rush. She winced in pain as he broke through, but the sensation dimmed as he went deep, deep into her. Immediately her body adjusted to his thick, long presence and a shock of pleasure shot through her belly like a shaft of sunlight.

She was so ready for him to start moving.

Except Gray didn't. He was utterly frozen. In the long period of motionless silence that followed, he didn't even seem to be breathing.

"Gray?" She ran her hands up his back. Sweat was running down his spine.

When he finally shifted his weight, it was to slowly withdraw from her. Inch by inch. Until he was out of her body.

And then he started to shake all over.

He grabbed the bedspread and yanked it off the floor, but his hands were trembling so badly, he fumbled as he tried to cover her up. When her body was no longer bare to him, he lay down next to her without touching her.

"Gray?" she said in the darkness. She could hear him breathing. And the tremors he was still racked by were transmitted through the mattress. "Gray?"

His hand gently stroked her hair back from her face. He was usually such a steady man, but his fingers were like leaves in the wind.

"Don't you want to…keep going?" she asked.

As he shook his head, she felt like bursting into tears.

"Then I should leave," she said, sitting up.

His arm came lightly around her waist. In spite of the strength she knew he had, he only applied a little pressure. The touch was like a request. And a humble one at that.

She lay back down. The arm slowly moved off her body, as if he didn't want her to feel trapped.

"I'm so sorry," he said. His voice was eerie. Strangled. With none of his usual arrogance or strength behind the words. "I'm so sorry I hurt you."

"Actually, it was—"

"Why didn't you tell me?" he asked softly.

"Would it have made a difference?"

"Of course it would have. I never would have taken you to bed if I'd known."

As if her virginity were a disease he didn't want to catch.

"Wow. That really makes me feel terrific."

He instantly took her hand. "You should have saved it for Tom."

Joy clenched her teeth. "If you bring him up one more time, I swear to God I'm going to scream."

"Fine. You should have saved it for someone who loved you."

Ouch.

"You know something, Gray, I think I really need to get going."

"No, stay. I promise I won't touch you again. I'd just be grateful if you'd…I'm afraid if you leave now, I'll never see you again, and I can't bear that."

"Listen to me," she said distinctly. "You didn't hurt me."

"I pushed you down on this bed. I threw your legs apart. And then I rammed myself inside of you." His voice thinned. "You're a vir—you were a virgin."

"I chose to be with you. I wanted you. You didn't do anything—"

"Don't you *dare* defend me," he growled. "This never should have happened."

She rolled over onto her back, thinking she disagreed.

Sure, he didn't love her. And yes, it would have been smarter to wait to make love for the first time with someone who did. But at this moment, she regretted the partial knowledge of him more than her decision to be with him in the first place.

Her body was aching from everything it had been promised and all it had been denied. Certainly, his was the same, too. Or had the idea that she'd never been with a man before been a total turnoff?

Damn. She was getting really good at shutting down his attraction to her, wasn't she? First the *I love you* fiasco. Now the virginity thing. Short of telling him she was pregnant, she figured she was almost out of shockers.

Yeah, well, it wasn't as if she had to worry about surprising him anymore. When was the next time she'd be anywhere near his sheets and blankets again?

"Sleep here tonight," he said.

She turned her head and looked across the pillow. She wished there was more light so she could read his expression better.

The thing was, she didn't want to go. She really didn't. Because maybe in the morning, they'd both make more sense. Maybe they could start over.

"Fine," she said. When she heard his breath release, she was surprised that her spending the night meant so much to him. "But, Gray?"

"Yeah?"

"This isn't over between us."

"I know. Believe me, I know."

GRAY WAITED UNTIL Joy's breathing was even before getting up and going to the bathroom. In the dark, he stripped the condom off of himself and flushed it, feeling like the worst kind of thug.

After he splashed some water on his face, he braced his hands against the sink and let his head hang loose.

God. Damn.

No miserable stunt he'd ever pulled in his life came close to what he'd done in that bedroom. All his other misdeeds were grains of sand. Numerous, but irrelevant in comparison.

When he'd barrel-assed into Joy's body, he hadn't been prepared for what he'd found. And he'd thrust so strongly, he hadn't been able to stop his body's momentum until he was deep inside of her. She'd been so tight, so good, so sweet. Even as horrible comprehension was dawning, a release like nothing he'd ever come close to had threatened to overcome him. He'd forced himself to be still, clenching the muscles in his body, squeezing his eyes shut. There'd been no way in hell he was going to let that pleasure out. Not after he'd hurt her like that.

It had taken a while until he'd been up to withdrawing and even his slow, measured retreat had pushed him back to the brink. When he was finally free of her, the torment of sexual denial had made him shake, the pain radiating out from his erection until he'd felt the sting in every hair on his head. But it couldn't have been worse than what he'd put her through.

Gray grabbed a towel and dried his face off.

He'd been so wrong about Joy. Or rather, he'd been right about her in the first place. And she had suffered for his mistake.

At least he knew exactly what he needed to do next.

CHAPTER NINE

THE NEXT MORNING Joy woke up alone in the big bed, still wrapped tightly in the comforter. Next to her, there was a deep indent on top of the duvet and a pillow wadded up into a ball.

She pushed her hair back, threw off the covers and got to her feet. When she returned from the bathroom in a robe, Gray was standing at the bed, fully clothed. And staring at the small spot of blood on the sheets.

He looked over his shoulder, eyes dilated.

"Are you okay?" he said roughly.

In a flash, she remembered what he'd felt like on top of her. Heavy, hard, strong. She was dying to have him again.

"Joy?"

"I'm perfectly fine."

His eyes traced over her body, but there was no heat in them. "May I bring you some breakfast?"

This was said as if she were a houseguest and not someone he'd been naked with the night before.

Joy shook her head. "I'm not hungry, but you can answer a question for me. How is it possible that we made love and now you look at me with clinical detachment?"

He closed his eyes, withdrawing even further. As if that were possible?

"First of all, that was sex last night. You deserved to

be caressed and worshiped and entered gently. All you got was laid and laid badly. I will never forgive myself. And secondly, my primary concern is taking care of you, not making you feel awkward because I'm a leering son of a bitch."

Joy put her hands on her hips, taking strength from frustration.

"You know, I really need you to ditch the hair shirt you've strapped on." Her voice was strong, direct. She couldn't believe she was talking to him with such authority. "I still want you. You gave me so little of what we both needed—"

"I gave you every inch and then some. Until you *bled.*"

"Will you let me finish? You pulled out so fast, I didn't even have a chance to get used to you. To feel you. I want to know what it's really like. With you."

"Someday, a man will love you rig—"

"Spare me the fairy tale, okay?" she snapped. "Just because I haven't had a lover before, doesn't mean I can't make my own decisions. I want you. I chose you."

"I didn't deserve the gift!" His voice boomed through the room, self-hatred rolling off him in waves.

"I think you did," she said quietly.

Gray leaned forward on his hips and spoke in a low, dangerous tone. "Then you don't know me well enough."

She thought of him refusing to let her ride home from his house in the dark on her bike. Of the respect he had for the way she treated her family with kindness. She remembered him lying beside her in the dark last night, his big body so tense as he pleaded with her to stay. She saw him staring down at the blood on the sheets just now, looking as if he were going to cry out.

He was a hard man. But never a bad one.

"You're wrong," she whispered. "I know you very well."

"No, you don't." He looked down at the bed again.

She went over and touched his arm. His body jerked and he stepped back from her.

"Don't."

Joy frowned. "Why not?"

"Because compassion from you is the last thing I want right now."

Pain cut through her chest, draining her burst of strength. Gathering up the lapels of the robe, she said in a small voice, "I'd like to get dressed now, if you don't mind."

He cursed. "I didn't mean it like that, Joy. It's just… you don't need to be taking care of me. You're the one who got hurt."

No, she thought. They were both aching this morning.

"Are you available at three o'clock today?" he asked.

"For what?"

"To see me."

"Why?"

"Please." His eyes held hers, as if he wanted to will her into saying yes. She had a feeling it was as close as he'd ever gotten to begging.

"Okay, but on one condition."

"Anything. You name it."

"Kiss me. Right now."

Gray's eyes flared. "Joy—"

"I'm serious. I want you to kiss me."

She had no idea where this strong woman thing was coming from. But she was going to go with it.

And evidently, so was he.

Gray slowly reached out, taking her face gently into his hands. His mouth brushed over hers. Lightly.

She wrapped her arms around his neck, bringing her body against his. "Like you mean it, Gray."

His eyes squeezed shut. The thick vein at his throat started throbbing from the hard pump of his blood and his lips parted as though he were having trouble finding his next breath.

Still, his touch stayed soft, his thumb stroking her cheek.

When his eyelids flipped open, she caught a quick glance of a surging, sexual burn. Then his head came down, his mouth hovering over hers without making contact. She could feel the coiled strength in him, the heat coming off of him. However conflicted his mind was about what had happened, his body was hard for her. Ready for her.

"I always mean it when I kiss you," he said with more gravel than voice.

His lips stroked hers once and then he strode out of the room.

Joy reached out for the wall to steady herself.

Frankly, she was impressed he could walk without a limp after that.

Damn it, the man had way too much self-control. And she wanted the very beast he refused to let out.

When he reappeared with her dress, he put it down on the bureau.

"May I call a car for you?" His voice was smooth as

an ice cube and just about as warm. As if that incandescent moment between them had never happened.

So this is sophistication in action, she thought. Here she was quaking in a bathrobe, while he waltzed around as though the last thing he'd done was read the newspaper.

Must be nice.

"I'll get a taxi myself," she muttered.

"I'd rather call my car—"

"I'm sure you would."

He hesitated in the doorway.

She wondered what he would do if she stepped out of the robe. Would he turn away? Probably. And though she wanted him like nothing else, she didn't need to get shut down by the man.

With one last look toward the bed, he stepped out of the room, shutting the door behind himself.

She wanted to yell out that his Prince Charming thing wasn't charming. Wasn't necessary. Was driving her flipping nuts.

Joy stripped the robe off, balled it up and pitched it at the double doors.

Man, she'd learned a nasty little lesson in the last twelve hours. When people had told her reality was never as good as a fantasy, she'd believed them on some level. She'd just been unprepared for how much the real thing sucked in comparison.

She'd actually been to bed with Gray, the man she'd worshiped for years, except she was still a virgin for all intents and purposes.

And he still wanted her, badly enough to shake from it, except now he wouldn't touch her.

Great.

Just terrific.

No wonder people liked fiction.

A LITTLE BEFORE three o'clock, Joy left Cass's penthouse and went down to wait for Gray on Park Avenue. It was an exceptional fall day with warm sunshine and a cool breeze, and after having spent hours working on the red gown, it felt good to be outside. She was just beginning to relax when a black limousine eased to a halt in front of the building. Gray emerged from the rear and smiled remotely as she walked over. He didn't touch her as she moved past him and slid inside.

"Did you have lunch?" he asked, getting in and shutting the door.

"Just some crackers and cheese." She stretched, easing her back. The limousine smelled like leather and Gray's aftershave. She tried to ignore how good the combination was.

"We'll go for tea afterward at the Pierre."

She looked at her black pants and the loose black blazer.

"You're perfectly dressed," he said. "You look beautiful."

She laughed tightly. "These clothes are off the rack. Really off the rack. I can't believe you mean that."

"I don't lie. It's one of my few virtues."

"What are the others?"

"I take responsibility for my actions."

She took a deep breath and looked out the window. An awkward silence cropped up between them, growing thicker as the limousine got stuck in traffic.

"Where are we going?" she asked.

"You'll see."

A little while later the car stopped on Fifth Avenue. Gray didn't wait for the driver to come around, but opened the door and stood at the curb himself. As she got out, she looked up at a towering, stone facade.

Tiffany's.

"What are we doing here?" she asked slowly.

"Come with me." He touched her elbow, ushering her through a pair of glass doors. As soon as they were inside the yawning space, a man in a three-piece suit came up to them.

"Mr. Bennett, good afternoon. Please, this way."

The only thing that stopped Joy from planting her feet and demanding to know what was going on was a fear that she was jumping to conclusions. No man, especially not Gray Bennett, asked a woman to marry him just because he took her virginity. No way. And how embarrassing would it be to blurt out that little misconception when all he wanted was her advice on a set of cuff links?

As they walked through a maze of glass cases, salespeople dressed like businessmen and women watched them, as if Gray's arrival was something extraordinary. Their smiles and nods to him were deferential. They flat-out stared in awe at Joy.

To avoid the looks, she kept her eyes on the sparklers lying in their see-through cages.

It was as though the place were some kind of jewelry zoo, she thought numbly.

When she hesitated at the elevators, she felt Gray take her hand. From then on, she barely tracked where they went in the building. She just followed along, swept up in some tide, thinking that God only knew where she was going to end up.

They were shown into a small room with a high ceiling. The furniture was minimal, but lovely, a mahogany table and three ornate, matching chairs, two on one side. A bouquet of fresh roses, in pale pinks and yellows, was arranged in a crystal bowl. The place smelled like a garden, but she wasn't calmed.

No, she wasn't calm at all. Her heart was beating like a bird's and she took her hand from Gray's because her palm was getting sweaty.

Gray indicated she should sit, which was just fine. Her knees were thinking of taking a break anyway. He took the chair beside hers, resting one arm on the table. She noticed absently that the white of his cuff screamed in contrast to the dark sleeve of his jacket.

During the ensuing silence, Joy downshifted from anxious into panic. And the suffocating sensation got worse when Three Piece came in with a thin leather box about eight inches long and four inches wide. The man flipped open the top and slid the tray forward.

Diamond rings.

She looked at Three Piece. His eyes glowed with pride at what he could offer.

Which was understandable considering you could light up a football stadium with what was shining out of that box.

"Will you excuse us?" she said to the man in a surprisingly commanding tone.

But that was the strength of insanity, she thought. Steady conviction backed up by nothing rational.

Three Piece nodded, as if she were his boss. "But of course."

While he left with a bow, she had a feeling he would

have taken a swan dive out the window if she or Gray had asked him to.

Commission. Clearly on commission. And what a bundle he could make moving one of those headlights, she thought.

When the door shut, she reached out and plucked a ring from its velvet sheath. The size was substantial. Absurd. And it was one of the smaller ones.

Beneath the overhead lighting, the stone's brilliance hurt her eyes. And surely there was a hell of a metaphor in that.

"What do you think you're doing?" She didn't look at Gray. Couldn't.

"Asking you to marry me."

She shook her head, but only because she felt like she needed to do something other than start crying. Destiny seemed so cruel. To put her this close to being his wife.

"Why?" she muttered to herself. "Why are you doing this to me?"

"Last night—"

"Oh, *please.*" God, she'd had it with his regrets. "Are you aware we're living in the twenty-first century? I mean, we've got electricity, cars, the internet—"

"Joy, listen to me—"

"And we've been through something called the sexual revolution—"

"Goddamn it—"

"Which, in case you're not familiar with what happened, made sex not such a big deal. So when you nail a virgin—"

Now he *really* cursed. A ringing, four-letter, tongue-burner.

"—you don't have to do something stupid. Like ask her to marry you."

"Are you finished?"

She cocked her head. Glared at him. "Actually, I'm just getting started. Why do you think in a million years—"

He grabbed her shoulders hard, nearly pulling her out of her chair. Gone was the polite restraint. His eyes burned. "I hurt you."

"And you think this is going to make it better? Gray, you don't mean this. You don't want this. You're flying wild on some huge guilt trip and as soon as you come down, you're going to hate what you've done. Worse, you're going to end up resenting the hell out of me and that'll do more damage than anything you did to my body last night."

He let her go, moving her gently back. "I just want to make it right. I want to make it up to you."

"Well, this isn't going to do it. I want to be chosen by my husband. Freely." Her voice threatened to break and she glanced away. To the roses.

And didn't they look just like a bridal bouquet? Terrific.

She fought against the urge to bury her face in her hands.

She wanted to be picked by Gray. She really did. And there was a part of her that was desperately tempted to give herself up to the mistake he was making.

Except she couldn't. There was no way to ignore the truth that, but for the fact she'd had no lover before him, they never, ever, would have been near those diamonds.

She put the ring back.

"Let's go," she said, suddenly exhausted.

He took her hand in his. "Are you sure you don't want one of those?"

"Under these circumstances? Absolutely not." She stared at the brilliant display. "Besides, they're beautiful, but rather cold."

"Will you still let me see you?" he said abruptly.

She looked over at him. A clean break would be in her best interests, especially because she couldn't begin to guess where they were headed. It wasn't as if he was into relationships.

"You can't be serious."

He cleared his throat, ignoring her comment. "It can be here, up north, wherever. I'll do the traveling. I'll come to you. I just want to keep seeing you, okay?"

She shook her head. "I'm not interested in hanging around just so you can work out your guilt. In fact, it's kind of insulting to think that's the only reason you'd want to see me."

"That's not why. I like you, I honestly do. I like being with you. You're…different to me."

"Yeah, I'll bet. When was the last time you had a v—" She shut her mouth. "Please don't answer that."

"Joy, look at me." She shifted her eyes over to his. "I'm not expecting anything from you. We can keep it as casual, as light, as you want."

She measured his eyes, surprised by the gravity in them. The need.

"I don't know, Gray."

As if her answer wasn't the one he wanted, he eyed the rings again.

She closed the lid on the box and got to her feet.

He stared up at her. "Most women would have taken one of those."

“I don’t doubt it.”

He shook his head. “You keep surprising me.”

She thought about the clarity with which she saw what he was doing even though she was hurting. And the strength that had allowed her to pull them both back from his lapse in judgment. It was odd. He was supposed to be the worldly, powerful one, but she had the sense that she was handling the situation, the emotions, better than he was.

“Funny, I’m kind of surprising myself, too.”

CHAPTER TEN

A WEEK LATER GRAY WATCHED as Joy walked into the Congress Club's bar. His blood pumped harder just seeing her. It was always like that. Anytime she came into sight. Anytime he smelled her. Anytime he thought about her.

To hell with exposure therapy. He wanted her more every day, not less, though he was keeping a leash on himself.

And he knew he was lucky. One of Cass's friends had seen some of Joy's work and ordered two gowns. Which meant Joy had had to stay in Manhattan even after she'd finished the dress for Cass. So he'd had a rare chance to see her on a regular basis.

He'd been with her almost every night, taking her to the theater, out to dinner, to a gallery opening. But at the end of each date, he left her at the lobby of Cassandra's building with nothing more than the request to see her the next day. He was never sure he would. He kept waiting for her to pull the plug on him, uncertain when he phoned Cass's that Joy would accept his call or even still be in town.

The combination of sexual frustration and newfound insecurity was driving him nuts. As a public service, every night he'd go back to the Waldorf, change into his workout clothes and hit the gym for hours. He was so sore from lifting, he could barely brush his teeth. And stairs were a challenge because he'd burned out his thighs on the treadmill.

At this rate he was going to end up with dentures and a walker. Prematurely.

When Joy caught sight of him, she gave him a little wave. As she came over to his table, other men watched her discreetly and eyed Gray with envy. He didn't appreciate either kind of attention. He didn't need to be reminded of how attractive other men found her.

"You are not going to believe this," she said as he helped her with a chair.

God, she was beautiful. Her hair was up tonight and her cheeks glowed from the cold wind blowing through the city.

He wanted to kiss her hello, but didn't. He'd been so careful not to touch her though the distance was nearly impossible to bear. Focusing on the pale line of her throat, he wanted to—

"Gray?"

"Sorry?"

She smiled at him. "I asked if you'd seen this."

He looked at what she was holding out to him. It was the Style section of the *New York Times.* There was a picture of Cassandra wearing a stunning red gown and the caption underneath had Joy named as the designer.

"Cassandra's dress was a hit at the gala! And four more of her friends want me to make gowns for them. Isn't this great?"

He smiled, enjoying her pleasure. Her pride. "I'm not surprised in the slightest."

"I'm going to see the women tomorrow morning and then go home and work on the gowns."

"Home? To Saranac Lake?" When she nodded, he frowned. "Do you have to leave?"

"I can't very well keep staying with Cass. She's been far too generous with that guest room already." As the bartender came over, she looked up. "I'd like a Chardonnay, please. Just the house."

The man nodded. "Another bourbon for you, Mr. Bennett?"

"No, I'm good." When they were alone, he said, "I have an extra bedroom. Would you like to stay with me?"

He almost hoped she'd say no. The idea of her sleeping across the suite from him was enough to make his skin itch.

"Thanks, but no. I have to go home. Grand-Em is better on her new meds, but they all need a break from watching her. And Nate and Frankie's wedding is in three weeks. I want to be there to help out." She leaned back as her wine was put down. "Thank you."

Gray stroked the side of his glass, trying to rearrange his schedule in his head. "I have to go to D.C. tomorrow, otherwise I'd drive you back."

"That's okay. I like the train."

"When will you return?"

A large shadow came over their table. "Hey, Bennett, what's doing?"

Gray looked up at Sean O'Banyon. The man was wearing a well-well-well-isn't-this-interesting expression.

"O'Banyon," Gray said, while shooting a warning glance at his friend. "I thought you were in Japan this week."

"Came back early. And who might you be?" the man murmured, looking at Joy.

"Joy Moorehouse," she answered, offering her hand and a smile.

"Joy? Nice name."

"Thank you," she said, as they shook.

"Mind if I join you?"

Now, that was a bad idea, Gray thought. "As a matter of fact, yes—"

"Of course not." Joy glanced across the table, obviously surprised at his rudeness.

As SOB took a seat, Gray reminded himself that the darkly handsome man was a good buddy. And not target practice.

"So, Joy, has Bennett been showing you a lot of the city?"

"Is it so obvious I'm not from here?"

SOB smiled, clearly determined to dust off his charm. The bastard. "No, I just recall my man mentioning that you lived up north."

Joy's eyes skipped across the table, as if she were surprised Gray had been talking about her.

Gray glowered. "Don't you have to be somewhere hocking stocks, O'Banyon? Like a widows and orphans convention?"

SOB laughed and ordered a whiskey.

"I've got plenty of time to spare. Unlike yourself. I hear Wright's got a shot in the mayoral election thanks to your magic." The man smiled across the table at Joy. "Has Bennett told you what he really does for a living?"

Gray nursed his bourbon. "She doesn't want to hear about that."

"Actually, I do," Joy said.

"No, you don't."

"Ah, Bennett's just being shy." SOB rolled right along. "He's a makeover artist. He turns people into whoever he needs them to be to get elected. I keep telling him if he gets tossed out of Washington, he could always pick up some tweezers and a tube of lipstick. You know, work the Chanel counter somewhere."

"I'm sure it's a lot more complicated than that," Joy said, glancing at Gray with expectation.

God, the idea of talking to her about what he did made him feel the proverbial dirt under his nails more than ever.

When he stayed quiet, she prompted, "And it must be so exciting."

"It isn't," Gray said briskly.

"Oh, come on," SOB shot back, "you're at the epicenter of American politics and I love your stories. Remember that time when—"

Gray's voice sliced right through his friend's words. "So, O'Banyon, I hear you're bringing out an IPO on one of Nick Farrell's companies."

There was a long pause.

Sean's eyes narrowed and Joy shifted in her chair.

And then thankfully the conversation veered in another direction as SOB went into a whole spiel on initial public offerings. Joy asked a lot of very insightful questions, and by the time Sean had polished off his whiskey, he was looking at her as if he were actually seeing her.

This rankled, of course, but Gray had to give his friend credit. No matter how lovely Joy was, O'Banyon never looked anywhere except in her eyes. And he didn't let his cutting humor hit on topics like men, women and relationships or Gray's job.

When SOB got up to leave, he shook Joy's hand, clapped Gray on the shoulder and sauntered off.

"It was nice to meet one of your friends," Joy murmured as she watched the man cut through the crowd. "Have you known him long?"

"Since college."

"Is he married?"

"O'Banyon? No way. That man's not going down the aisle unless there's a shotgun involved. And the business end's pointed at his head."

"Oh. Well, it sounds like he works a lot."

"He's one of the best investment bankers in town."

"Doesn't he get lonely sometimes?"

Gray laughed. "Trust me, if he spends the night by himself, it's his choice. He's got more women than he knows what to do with."

Joy seemed chastened, looking down into her wineglass.

"When are you coming back to the city?" Gray asked.

"Why don't you want to tell me about your work?"

Gray frowned. "Don't listen to O'Banyon. It's not that interesting. So when are you coming back?"

She stayed silent.

"Joy?"

"Is it because I'm not sophisticated?"

"Sophis—no, not at all." He simply was not in a big hurry to tell her about the things he'd done. The threats he'd made. The threats he'd followed through on.

"Then why?"

"It's just not relevant." He wanted to reach across

the table and take her hand. "Now, tell me, when will you be back?"

She hesitated, as if debating whether or not to let the subject drop. "After the wedding."

Had she said her sister was getting married in three weeks? That was so long. Too long.

"I'll come up to Saranac Lake before then," he said. "If you'll let me see you."

Joy moved her wineglass from side to side, sliding it over the table's glossy surface, the little Congress Club napkin under its base acting as a sled.

"Will you let me?" Gray pressed, aware that his whole body was tight. The idea that she would go up north and disappear terrified him for some reason. "Joy?"

She slowly nodded her head. "Yes. I'll see you."

"Good," he murmured, relaxing.

"But I have to be honest, I wish I could say no. I wish I didn't care whether or not I ever ran into you again. Actually, I wish I didn't want to see you at all." She frowned. "That sounds like an insult, but I don't mean it to be."

"Doesn't matter. As long as you want me. Want to see me, rather."

"Oh, I want you, all right," she said wryly. The blush that followed suggested she'd spoken without thinking and wished she could take the words back.

His eyes locked onto her lips. He remembered how soft they were. What they felt like against his. He imagined his tongue slipping into her mouth, penetrating, stroking.

"Gray?" she whispered. Her eyes widened, as if

she'd guessed where his thoughts had headed and he'd surprised her.

He kicked back his drink, draining the last inch in the glass. "Let's go in to dinner."

While they ate, Joy seemed quiet, or maybe he was the one who wasn't talking much. Whereas his mouth wasn't working, though, his eyes were pulling overtime. He couldn't stop staring at her, as if he were storing up memories for the next couple of weeks when he wouldn't be able to see her as much.

And the preoccupation got worse as they went back to Cassandra's in the limousine.

God, the idea she was leaving felt all wrong to him.

"Will you call me as soon as you're home so I know you got up north safely?" he said.

"Sure."

The car paused at a stoplight.

"I'm going to miss you, Joy."

She looked across the seat as if he'd astonished her. And then she shocked the hell out of him.

She leaned forward, put her hands on his chest and kissed him softly on the mouth.

The brush of her lips against his was like getting whipped. As his body surged, he gripped her upper arms, getting caught between the urge to drag her on top of him and the memory of how he'd hurt her before.

He carefully forced her back a little. "Joy…"

"I can feel you tremble. Why are you pushing me away?"

He didn't trust himself to speak. Because if he opened his mouth, he was just as likely to lick the skin of her neck.

When he stayed silent, she fought against his hold,

her palms working their way into his jacket, onto his pecs. His body jerked reflexively, his hips popping off the seat and begging for any part of her. Her hands. Her mouth.

Dear God, her mouth.

"Do you shake because you want me, Gray? Or is it something else?"

"Sweet woman…" he groaned.

"Please, I need to know. You've hardly touched me since…that night. I don't know what we're doing on these dates. Do you still want me?"

He let go of her arms and cupped her face. "Let's not talk about that—"

"Do you?"

"Joy—"

"Fine. I'll find out for myself." With a quick movement, her hand went down between his legs and settled on his heavy arousal.

His head flipped back against the seat and a moan broke out of him.

"Good Lord," she whispered. "Gray, why are you denying us?"

He tried to peel her hands off of him and the friction of her wanting to stay with his body while he attempted to move her away was beyond pleasure. The rubbing, the heat, the knowledge that it was her hand on him, it all took him right to the edge of release. He clenched his teeth as sweat broke out across his forehead.

"Stop it," he said, taking control. He forced her back against the seat using his strength and weight advantage. He was panting like a dog and rabid like one, too. "We're not going to do this in the back of a limo. I've already treated you like a whore once, I'm not going to do it again."

Her eyes glittered up at him. "How long are you going to penalize us for a mistake you didn't make?"

"Until I don't want to get sick every time I think about it."

While he smoothed her hair back, her lips parted as if she was ready for his kiss. Looking down at her, he thought it was quite possible he would never see anything more lovely. Her cheeks were tinted with the high color of feminine desire, her chest was moving up and down in an uneven rhythm, the heat of her body was coming through her clothes into his.

"You're so beautiful right now," he said in a guttural voice. "You take my damned breath away."

He couldn't help himself. He put his mouth on hers, swallowing her sigh of satisfaction. But as much as it killed him, he kept the kiss light.

"I want you. Never doubt that," he said. "All you have to do is look at me and I'm hard, ready, starved. I can't remember what it's like not to ache."

He rolled off of her, moving back to his own side of the seat. With a wince, he rearranged himself in his pants and then put his head in his hands. The pain of wanting her was sharp and shiny as a blade, bearing deep into the muscles of his thighs, making his back spasm. He tried to keep as still as possible because even the slightest shift of his boxers had him grinding his molars.

"I'll come up the weekend after next," he muttered. "Because as much as it hurts to be around you, it's worse when I don't see you."

WHEN JOY BOARDED her train the following afternoon and picked a place to sit, she figured she had two things going for her: she had a window seat and the car was full of businessmen. For the next three hours, the view of the Hudson River would be a welcome distraction and the relentless flipping of newspapers was better than the howls of bored, cranky children.

Although to be truthful, she was feeling something close to colicky herself.

Her meetings with Cassandra's friends had gone well enough. The women were clear about what they liked, but not rigid. The timelines were reasonable. And the pay was outrageously good. As with Cass, the give and take as designs were discussed was something Joy really liked and the faith that the clients had in her sense of style was a compliment the likes of which she'd never had before.

So she should be happy. And she was. But as the train emerged from the Penn Station tunnel system and trundled past the high-rise apartment buildings and the projects, she felt as though she was leaving something important in the city.

Gray.

God, she missed him already. Even though she had no idea what she was to him. Did they have a relationship? She wasn't sure. He called her, took her out, treated her with kid gloves and the utmost respect. But he never talked about feelings, or the future, or where they were going. It was, she supposed, like dating a ghost. When they were in front of you, they had your total attention. When they disappeared, you realized how little of them you'd seen.

Shaking her head, she flipped through the most recent issue of *Vogue* with quick fingers and careless eyes. She barely noticed the clothes, taking more interest in jettisoning the subscription flyers and ripping out the perfumed inserts that made her sneeze.

From across the aisle, she heard the soft, electronic dialing of a cell phone. She glanced over as a businessman put some NASA-worthy silver gadget up to his ear. The guy must have been in his late twenties, just like her, but he seemed way out of her league with his Wall Street clothes and his stylish, dark-rimmed glasses.

"Hey," the guy said softly. "I'm glad you got my message. No, nothing. I was just calling to see how you're doing."

Joy looked away, trying not to eavesdrop.

"Today was awful, but thanks for asking." He laughed. "You're sure you want the gory details?" Another chuckle. "Okay…"

Definitely talking to his wife. Sharing his life with her.

Joy shifted in her seat. Crossed and then recrossed her legs. She tried to imagine Gray unloading his stress the way the guy across the aisle was doing with his woman. She couldn't.

In the past week, Gray had reestablished himself as a great listener and a lousy talker. He always asked how she'd spent her time, where she'd gone, who she'd seen. But he never volunteered anything about himself. And when she inquired about his day? Like the politicians he worked with, he always gave her a smooth, solicitous, empty answer.

Last night at the bar, she'd been so hopeful when his friend had brought up Gray's work. But then he'd changed the topic. Sternly.

The man across the aisle laughed again. "You're right. I probably shouldn't have gotten on my high horse. But the guy was undermining me in front of—I know. Yeah."

The respect in his voice was hard to hear.

Joy looked down at her lap and realized she'd linked her fingers together and was sitting up straight. It was a pose right out of Grand-Em's old-fashioned playbook. The proper way for a lady to sit.

As if good posture might make her worthy of being Gray's confidante.

How pathetic.

With a series of jerks and shuffles, she tried to loosen herself up and to not dwell on how Gray saw her. The former was a success as she curled one leg under her butt and slouched against the window. The latter was an abject failure.

When she'd pressed him on why he wouldn't talk about his work, afraid that he didn't think she was sophisticated enough, all he'd said was no, that wasn't it. Which was not the same thing as, *No, you are not hopelessly provincial and incapable of understanding the big, bad sandbox I play in.* It just meant there was another reason he kept to himself other than her being simpleminded.

Which she knew she was. At least compared to him and the kinds of people he was used to. After all, she hadn't come to him as a woman of the world, but as a virgin from the sticks.

God, when she thought of it like that, what in good heavens had given her the confidence to get into his bed in the first place? Or to stand up to him the following morning? Or to turn him down at Tiffany's?

Certainly she'd done all of those things. It just seemed, as the train got farther and farther from the city, she couldn't remember how.

Maybe there was something in the Manhattan water. Like a mineral that activated the brain's chutzpah receptors.

"About twenty minutes," the businessman was saying. "Which is a godsend. I'm half asleep as it is."

Joy pictured the woman on the other end of the call and wanted to be that person in Gray's life. The one he sought out for counsel. The one he called when he was unsure. The one he held at night—

"I love you, Mom," the man said as he hung up.

Okay, strike that. She didn't want to be Gray's mother.

But she would have loved the opportunity to be his equal. His partner.

Although that wasn't likely to happen anytime soon. He wanted her, but he wasn't willing to take her to bed. He liked her well enough, but affection wasn't love. He felt badly for treating her as he had, but that was hardly a basis for a relationship.

And as she'd told him, fielding his regrets wasn't something she was interested in.

After all, how many romantic movies had the hero and heroine embracing in the rain, their future finally clear as the man whispers, *I guilt you, I truly, truly guilt you.*

Yeah, right. Now there was a happy-ever-after.

So the question was, Why was she holding on?

Hope, she thought. Hope and…love.

There was just something that drew her to him. And that pull was making her resent every mile that took her farther north.

She wiggled around, drumming her fingers on the armrest. As the city receded and the suburbs began to dominate the landscape, she thought it was a little bizarre that she now knew how to get around the Big Apple. Sure, she was far from being a native, but she was familiar with the basic layout of the streets and avenues and the locations and characters of the different neighborhoods.

Heck, the Flat Iron District now meant something to her. And she could actually find it without a map. Although why Sixth Avenue had to be called the Avenue of the Americas she couldn't understand. And circumnavigating the subway system was still a little scary.

She actually wanted to be pounding the pavement right now, heading to the garment dealers to look at samples. She'd grab a deli sandwich on the run and eat it quickly. Maybe stop later for some Zabar's coffee that she could take out onto the street with her. She'd rush along with the other pedestrians, visions of the gowns she would make for her clients filling her mind.

As night fell, she would meet Gray for dinner at some interesting, out-of-the-way restaurant. And this time, when he took her home, he would kiss her. Come upstairs with her. Stay until morning.

By the time the train pulled into the Croton/Harmon station, and the young businessman got off, she realized she didn't want to go home. At all.

The reticence struck her as a betrayal.

But if she was honest, heading toward White Caps made her feel as though she was strapping on a yoke. Or stepping into clothes that no longer fit. She didn't want to go back to being the younger sister of super-competent Frankie. The sole keeper of Grand-Em. The one who'd missed and now worried so much about Alex. She didn't want to be the good old reliable, never-ruffle-the-feathers, follow-the-rules, Joy Moorehouse.

She much preferred being a woman in the big city. Who was starting up a new business. Who was free to go where she wanted, when she wanted, without worrying about who would cover for her with an elderly person. She wanted to be that person who could tell Cassandra Cutler what would look good and be right about it. Who could find her way around New York and be comfortable in the back of a taxi all by herself.

Most of all, she wanted to go back to being a lover capable of making Gray Bennett burn until he lost his voice.

She buried her face in her hands, feeling selfish. Frankie had given up so much to become a parent after their mother and father had died. Grand-Em hadn't asked to lose her faculties and she deserved to be cared for properly by someone who loved her as Joy did. And Alex needed support now, even if he shrank from it.

Maybe it wasn't that she didn't want to see her family. Maybe she just wanted them to see her in a different light.

Until recently, it was as if she'd gone through life as a kite in the wind. Tethered to her family, to White Caps, she'd skated this way and that, never choosing her direction, just responding to the currents. She'd taken business courses in college out of necessity, not because they interested her. She'd known the B&B was losing money and a practical major would mean she could get a higher-paying job and help out more. And while she was at UVM, she'd worked those jobs to save on living expenses, foregoing all that dating and partying. After graduation, she'd come home and cared for Grand-Em because their grandmother desperately needed help and there wasn't enough income to support a nurse.

Put in that context, it seemed like designing a dress for Cassandra was the first thing she'd chosen to do.

Well, that and giving herself to Gray.

CHAPTER ELEVEN

WHEN THE TRAIN PULLED into the Albany station, Joy dreaded getting off. Leaving the railcar made her feel as though she were cutting ties with the new parts of herself she'd discovered down in the city.

But then she looked out of the window and saw Frankie.

Her sister was scanning the passengers as they disembarked onto the platform. Dressed in a pair of blue jeans and an Irish knit sweater so big it must have been Nate's, she was so achingly familiar, so beautifully the same. She was home and comfort and stability.

Joy felt tears spike her lashes as she jostled her suitcase and portfolio down the aisle. How could she not want to be with her family? How could she even think of leaving them behind?

She blinked quickly, not wanting her emotions to show, but the instant Frankie made eye contact with her, Joy's vision went blurry again.

Frankie came running up, all smiles as she reached out to take some of the luggage burden. "Hey! I'm so glad—what's wrong?"

Joy put down her things and threw her arms around her sister. Frankie's hug back was so like her. Strong, secure, warm. She smelled like Ivory soap and fresh air.

"Joy, are you okay?"

Oh, God, Frankie. I made love with a man for the first time while I was away. With Gray. I'm scared that I really do love him and I'm going to get my heart crushed.

And I'm learning things about myself that seem to take me away from you and Alex and Grand-Em. From everything I've always known.

I fear I don't know who I am anymore. Or where I fit in. Or where I'm going.

"Joy?"

"I'm fine. Just glad to see you." Joy pulled back and wiped her eyes. "Sorry."

"For what?" Frankie bent down and picked up the suitcase. "There's nothing wrong with leaking, you know."

Joy grabbed the portfolio off the cement platform and followed her sister through the terminal. She took refuge in asking familiar questions. "How's Grand-Em?"

"She's doing so much better. I can't believe it. She's able to be still and occupied now for longer stretches of time. She can sit at the kitchen table and leaf through her diaries even while Nate's making noise at the stove. As a matter of fact, he's taken to watching her while he cooks and she seems to enjoy the smells in the kitchen."

"That's wonderful," Joy said as they stepped outside. "Are there any side effects yet?"

"She gets drowsy about an hour after she takes the pill. But other than that, she seems to be adjusting fine."

Joy felt some of her unease lift. If she was going to make those other dresses, she'd need to go back and forth to the city with some regularity. Her absences seemed more excusable if the burden on her family wasn't as great.

"And Alex?"

Her sister grew quiet as they wound their way through the parking lot.

"Frankie? What about Alex?"

"He needs another operation on his leg."

"Oh…God. When is he scheduled to go in?"

"This week."

"I'm glad I came back."

Frankie stopped in front of her old Honda Accord. "So am I. He's—uh, he's not doing too well. I've tried to talk with him so many times that he doesn't hear me anymore. Maybe you can give it a shot. He's barely eating anything and I know he doesn't sleep because his light stays on all night. I want to get him to a grief counselor, but he just won't have it."

"I'm not surprised."

"He did tell me he was happy you were coming home. I think he misses you. The two of you have always had that special connection."

They got in and Frankie started the car. "Hey, did I tell you what happened to Stu?"

During the two-hour drive up into the Adirondacks, all sorts of Saranac Lake news was imparted, and as her sister talked, Joy found herself absorbing the landscape. Interstate 87, also known as the Northway, was a four-lane highway running up New York State's vertical flank and it was familiar to her in the way only roads driven over when you were a child could be. She knew all the exits, all the grassy, tree-strewn medians, every mountain and body of water.

The deeper upstate they went, the more the restlessness she'd felt on the train drifted away, especially as they passed Glens Falls, the last enclave that could be considered a big-ish town. From then on, the exits got farther and farther apart. And she got closer and closer to home.

By the time they pulled up to White Caps, she was excited to be back. Looking forward to seeing Grand-Em. Eager to give Alex a hug, if he'd let her.

As she got out of the car, she took a deep breath. Cold, clean air shot into her sinuses, burning the lethargy of travel away. And it was so quiet that her soft sigh was loud enough to bring Frankie's head around.

Joy looked to the left, down to the lake. The water was nearly still, the lakeshore breeze only teasing the red and orange leaves of the oaks by the dock.

"You seem glad to be back," Frankie murmured.

"I am. Although part of me didn't want to leave the city."

"I can imagine. New York's an electric kind of place."

"Yes, it is." Joy glanced at White Caps.

Through the kitchen's picture window, she saw Nate and his best friend and *sous chef*, Spike, grinning like madmen while arguing over a steaming loaf of bread. All around them, everything in the room was as it always had been. The battered oak table was in the alcove, its matching chairs tucked under its flat back. There was a pile of mail on a counter next to some Macintosh apples in a wooden bowl. African violets were lined up on the windowsills.

"It's like I never left," Joy whispered, wondering whether she would get sucked back into her old role and how much she would mind it.

"Let's get inside," Frankie said, lifting the suitcase out of the back seat. "It's cold and you've only got that thin blazer on."

The minute they walked into the house, the men cheered.

"Hey! It's our world traveler," Spike called out while walking around the island. The man was well over six feet tall with tattoos on his neck and a muscular build that made you want to stick on his good side. His jet-black hair was spiked off his scalp. Thus his name. And his clothes were all dark and loose.

His appearance was scary as hell. But as he looked at her, his smile was pure gold and his odd, yellow eyes held deep affection. Well, affection and the kind of territoriality she imagined pit bulls and mastiffs had in spades. She had every confidence that if anyone ever messed with her, Spike would take care of the problem. And then some.

He held out his arms. "Show us some love, baby girl."

She laughed and gave him a hug. He always smelled good. Like clean laundry.

"Who's your new friend?" she asked, nodding to the unfamiliar stove.

Nate winked at her in greeting. "Old one died three days ago. We were lucky to take this gal off the showroom floor, but I'm not sure she's right for us."

Spike shook his head. "That damn thing ruined my bread."

"Yeah, the oven temperature's uneven."

"So tell us about the big city," Spike said while pushing her down into a chair. A minute later he'd poured her some juice from the fridge and put a plate of home-made wheat crackers in front of her. "I made these this afternoon. I think you'll like 'em."

As she shared some of her adventures, Nate cooked up some beef stew while the four of them laughed and chatted. They were just sitting down to dinner when the phone rang.

"I'll get it," Frankie said, jogging out to the office. She came back, a curious expression on her face. "Joy, it's for you. Gray Bennett."

Joy covered up her blush by wiping her mouth with a napkin and hustling out of the kitchen. She straightened her shirt before picking up the phone.

"Hello?"

"Why didn't you call me?" Gray demanded. Then he blew out a breath. "Sorry, that's not the best way to start a conversation, is it?"

She laughed. "I was going to give you a ring after we finished dinner."

"Was the trip okay?"

"Long. Gave me time to think."

There was a pause. "That can be dangerous."

"It wasn't."

"So what were you thinking of?"

Now it was her turn to be quiet. "Nothing important."

Wimp, she thought.

"Actually, that's not true," she amended. "I was thinking about how much I liked being down in the city. Spending some time away from home was a good thing, although I'm happy to be back. Well, happy and a little disoriented."

That's enough, she thought. She was wading into the babbling pool and it was better not to go into all the other things she'd thought over. The things involving him.

"Joy?"

"Yes?"

"I miss you." Before she could say anything, he went on. "I'll let you get back to your family, but I'll call you tomorrow."

She hugged herself, feeling a kind of happiness that cut so deep she knew it was dangerous. She'd been worried he'd forget her when she left, but it sure didn't sound as though he had. Of course, it had only been a matter of hours.

"I miss you, too, Gray."

"Oh, and one more thing."

"Yes?"

"See you in my dreams tonight," he said with a husky drawl.

And then he hung up.

When she sat back down at the table, she couldn't hide her grin, and conversation ground to a halt.

"What was that all about?" Frankie asked.

"Nothing."

"Yeah, right," Nate said, frowning. "Is Bennett making a play for you? 'Cause if he is, he better clean up his act."

"I thought you liked him," Joy murmured, smile fading.

"I do. I just know him too well. That man's a menace with women."

Joy played with her stew and thought about Gray's frustrating self-control. "He's been a real gentleman with me."

And who'd have thought that'd be a pity?

Nate stared across the table at her, his eyes flashing all sorts of male protective stuff. "Well, if he behaves himself, I'll let him keep his teeth."

Spike crossed his thick arms and nodded. "Wise man'll take you up on that offer. Dentures are rough and caps are expensive."

Joy shook her head and laughed, but she didn't get into bed with a smile on her face. Staring up at the ceiling, she wondered where Gray was and what he was doing. Somehow she couldn't picture him out with another woman, but how much of that was just wishful thinking?

She was turning over when she heard a soft knocking.

"Hello?" she called out. The door opened, revealing a big, dark shape. "Alex?"

She sat up as her brother limped into the room. He was leaning heavily on his crutches, his shoulders cocked out of place from bearing his weight. He had on a Red Wings T-shirt and a pair of flannel pajama bottoms.

"Sorry if I woke you," he said.

"I wasn't sleeping. And even if I was, you can come in whenever—"

"I wanted to thank you for the gift. When I saw the book on the bureau, I figured it had to be from you."

"You were asleep when I popped my head in. I didn't know if you still liked Harry Potter or whether you'd read that one."

"I do. And I didn't have it. So thanks."

"You're welcome."

He shuffled over to her worktable, staring down at the spools of thread and the pincushions. He reached out and picked up her pinking shears. "Tell me about the city."

"It was wonderful."

"Yeah? I was hoping you'd enjoy yourself. It's about time."

"And I have more clients now."

"Good for you." He put down the scissors, swaying a little on the crutches.

"Would you like to sit?" she asked.

He shook his head. "I'm trying to force myself to get up and around. Although this week is going to set me back again."

"What are they going to do to you?" she whispered, her hand coming up to her throat.

"The titanium rod they put in to replace the bone isn't taking. They're going to try again. If it doesn't work, I may be looking at amputation."

Joy hissed. "Alex—"

"I haven't told Frankie about that last part. Would appreciate if you didn't mention it to her."

She nodded. "Okay."

"And I shouldn't have told you. I guess I just wanted someone else to know. So not everyone would be knocked out if I come through this missing my lower leg."

He moved slowly over to the window and stared out into the dense night.

"Alex, is there anything I can do?"

He was silent. When he finally spoke, his voice was so soft, she could barely make out the words.

"Tell me how she is."

Joy leaned forward on the bed, as if she could better

understand what he wanted if she were closer to him. "I'm sorry—who?"

There was a long pause. "Cassandra."

Her brother's back was rigid, his bunched shoulders set tight as the cast on his leg. The still silence of him told her how important any information about the widow was.

"She's…ah, she's…I don't really know." Joy shifted her legs up and put her arms around her knees. "I didn't know her before and I don't know her all that well now. She doesn't sleep, I can tell you that. I'd hear her walking around the apartment at night. And I think she has to work at being social. Sometimes when we were out, I'd find her staring off into the crowd as if her body was in the room but she was somewhere else. And I caught her crying once. I got home early and she was out on the terrace, watching a cloud bank come in over the city. When she came back in, her eyes were red and she went into the library."

"Is that portrait of Reese still in there?"

"Yes."

Alex shook his head. "I used to razz him about that painting, but he said Cassandra needed something to remind her of him when he was gone."

There was a tight silence.

"She asked about you," Joy murmured.

Alex's head dropped down, his chest expanding as he took a deep breath. "What did you say?"

"Nothing. I figured you wouldn't want me telling her anything."

"Thank you. Thank you for that." He looked over his shoulder. "You've always understood me, haven't you?"

Joy shrugged. "Not always. But I respect your need for privacy."

He hobbled over and sat on the bed. Even though he'd lost weight, the springs groaned as they accepted him. He stretched his left leg out and winced.

"Is she seeing anyone?" he asked roughly.

"No."

He closed his eyes as if in relief, but then his expression hardened.

"It's still early. She'll find someone. A woman like her in New York can have her pick of men."

"She told me she wasn't interested in dating."

"That will change."

Joy studied her brother's face. The bitterness seemed out of place, she thought. Unless Alex was thinking of his friend.

"She seems to really miss her husband," Joy said. "And I don't think she's the kind of woman who's going to fill the void with a casual affair."

She'd hoped to relieve his mind. Instead, Alex's profile only grew tighter.

Something like an instinct or a premonition made her stop talking. What if Alex had feelings for… Good Lord.

"Why won't you see her?" Joy asked gently.

"I can't."

"Why?"

He shook his head sharply. "It's not right."

With a quick movement, Alex lifted one of his crutches into the air and stood it upright on the center of his palm, balancing the length on its rubber foot. The ease with which he pulled off the feat was typical of him. The marvelous hand-to-eye coordination, the control of his limbs. He'd always been good at anything physical, a consummate athlete.

She thought about what the loss of his lower leg would do to him. Heck, even if he could keep it, he might well be finished in the professional sailing game. The doctors had told him the limb would never be as strong as it had been.

She tried to imagine the black hole he was facing if he didn't go back to racing. Everything he had lived for would be lost: his profession; his colleagues; the outlet for his competitive spirit. And worst of all, his wanderlust, once slacked by the sea, would be earthbound.

Joy stroked his shoulder. "I love you, Alex. And no matter what happens, I'll always be there for you."

The crutch pitched off his hand, falling into thin air. He caught it before it landed on the ground.

"I love you, too," he said without looking at her.

CHAPTER TWELVE

JOY SPENT THE WEEK sketching, watching Grand-Em and, rather pathetically, waiting for Gray to call. The saving grace of the latter was at least he always did. Once in the morning. Once at night. Every single day, without fail.

He always asked about what she was doing. How the dresses were going. How her family was. His voice sounded good in her ear, and when he'd laugh softly or say her name, she was reminded of what it was like to be close enough to his body to feel him breathe.

She was never certain where he was, though, because mostly he called on his cell phone. A lot of the time she could hear people talking in the background. Or the drawling echoes of airport terminal announcements. Or the rush of wind, as if he were walking outside. She told herself it was enough that he called at all, but knew that wasn't true. Their time on the phone brought into focus what she wanted from him, and unfortunately, she suspected it was way too much.

He hadn't brought up the subject of coming to see her again.

The limbo was killing her and she knew they had to talk. It was harder to almost be with him, to almost be in a relationship, than not to see him at all. When she went back to New York after the wedding, she was going to make him sit down and they were going to have it out, face-to-face.

It wasn't a conversation she was looking forward to. After all, what had Frankie always said about men? If you have to ask the question, you aren't going to like the answer.

When Friday night rolled around, the week seemed to have passed at a crawl. Fortunately, Alex's surgery had gone as well as could be expected, but everyone at White Caps was tense. With all Alex had been through as well as the upcoming nuptials, distraction was the name of the game. Nate had burned himself reaching into the oven to take out a roast. Spike had taken a hunk out of his finger. Frankie had burst into tears when she'd gotten a card in the mail from an old friend.

And Joy? She was just a zombie.

They all needed a break and as the sun set, she was determined to get Nate and Frankie out of the house. They deserved it. And she was looking for a little time by herself.

"I don't know about this," Frankie said, pulling on her coat with Nate's help.

Joy walked over and opened the kitchen door, letting the heat rush out and the cold come in. She knew the shocking loss of BTUs would get her sister in gear more than anything else would.

"You two need to go on a date," Joy said. "When was the last time you were alone together while you were both awake?"

"August." Frankie eyed the open door, as if watching dollar bills walk out into the great outdoors. "Uh, could you shut the—"

"Go. Now."

"If Alex calls from the hospital—"

"He won't. He's fine. You talked to him an hour ago."

"But Spike's still at that motorcycle rally—"

"Frankie, I'm not twelve. I can handle being home by myself."

When the two finally left, Joy let her breath out and leaned back against the door. With Grand-Em asleep upstairs, the house was silent and she was so grateful.

Maybe that was part of her attraction to New York. There, she'd had the opportunity to be quiet, get lost in her sketching, let her mind wander.

Heading for the front of the house, she walked out of the kitchen through a pair of flap doors and surveyed the dining area. One side of the thirty-five-by-forty room was a jungle of tables and chairs, the other was barren. As they had just closed for the season, the rug was halfway shampooed, smelling of fake lemon. In a couple of days, after the low-nap pile was dry, they'd shuffle everything across the floor and finish the job.

After propping the flap doors open to help air the place out, she walked around the other public rooms of the house. The study was her favorite. Wallpapered in hunter green and black, filled with old books and Victorian knickknacks, the small space had always seemed like some kind of forest refuge. In the summer, you could open wide the diamond-paned windows and catch a fragrant breeze of lilacs and fresh water. In the cold months, there were usually logs ablaze in the fireplace, the smell of wood and leather filling the air.

Joy went over to the mahogany mantelpiece and inspected a collection of precious and absurd family heirlooms: silver trophy cups from crew races long since won; a stuffed bird of prey that had been rescued and cherished as a pet in the 1920s; a gnarled root from an oak tree that bore an astonishing resemblance to Elvis's profile. She fingered the objects, remembering her father having done the same thing.

Outside, the wind came up from the lake and rattled the house's shutters. On impulse, she lit the logs set in the hearth, watching as flames licked up the squat oak lengths. Sitting in her father's favorite leather wing chair, she felt the past wrap around her like a blanket, fond memories offering her gentle comfort.

She thought of how she'd dreaded coming back while she'd been on the train. Now, though, the city seemed far, far away. And as she imagined returning to Manhattan, she felt lost, caught somewhere between the new Joy and the old one.

It must have been an hour later when her stomach growled. She went into the kitchen, took a pan down from the hanging rack and got out some of Nate's stew to be reheated. Firing up the new stove was a trial. With the number of dials on the damn thing, she figured she could have landed a jet plane with all the options she had.

When the flame was finally set as low as it could go, she went back to check on the fire. She was putting another log on when she heard what sounded like a pounding noise in the back of the house.

Wiping her palms off on her blue jeans, she jogged to the kitchen door. There was a dark shape looming on the other side and she flipped the exterior light on before unlocking anything.

"Gray!" She fumbled with the knob. When she threw open the door, the cold wind came in with him. "What are you doing here?"

He looked exhausted, his pin-striped suit wrinkled, his collar open, his tie hanging loose. With tired eyes, he stared down at her face as if it had been ages since they'd parted.

"I had to see you," he said.

On impulse, she put her arms around him, feeling his body stiffen only briefly before he returned the embrace. He smelled divine. Just as she remembered. Sandalwood and cedar and…Gray.

"I was just sitting in front of the fire," she said. "Would you like to warm up a little?"

"Sounds ideal. And I'd love a drink. Traffic out of Albany was horrible."

She fixed him a bourbon, finding it hard to believe he'd come all the way to see her, and they headed into the study. He went straight to the fire, leaning on the mantelpiece, sipping the drink while staring into the flames. As she sat back down in the wing chair, she measured his tense profile.

"Is there something wrong?" she asked softly.

He jerked as if she'd startled him and then turned around. After a hesitation, he set down his drink and removed his suit jacket. As he laid it on the back of a chair, he took something out of the pocket. A small cloth bag.

"I've brought you a present." He came over to her. "Hold out both your hands."

She cupped her palms together as he undid a string and tipped the bag over. A sprinkling of shiny, black beads fell out.

No, they were buttons. Antique, jet buttons. Probably from the Victorian era.

"Gray, these are exquisite! Where did you find them?"

She fingered the glittering jumble. There were at least twenty, enough to run down the back of a dress.

"I was down in the garment district this week and passed a button store. I thought of you when I saw these in the window. Figured maybe you could use them on something."

She looked up at him. "Thank you."

He nodded. And then reached out, brushing her cheek with his forefinger.

"Gray, what's going on?"

Abruptly he sank to his knees in front of her. "Can I hold you?"

"Of course—"

He put his hands on the insides of her knees and gently separated her thighs. Then he nestled his big body against her, wrapping his arms around her back and putting his cheek against her breastbone. She felt his breath leave on a low sigh.

Not knowing what else to do, she stroked his hair.

Even though she didn't want him to be upset, she was grateful that he was letting down his guard a little. That he'd come to her. She figured when he was ready, he would talk, and until then she was content to just hold him.

Joy pressed her lips to the top of his head, running her hands across his shoulders, feeling the fine cotton of his business shirt like silk over his muscles.

Oh, she was so content just to hold him.

GRAY LET HIMSELF sink into Joy, thinking he'd never had a haven, a place to go when he was exhausted with life. Usually when things got overwhelming, he went out with O'Banyon or other friends of that ilk, business leaders who drank hard and talked tough because they were hard, tough men.

On the whole, it had been a damn good strategy for staying sharp. Self-medicating with bourbon and testosterone had kept him from dwelling on his weaknesses, the things that frightened him, his anxieties about the future or the present or the past. And he'd liked that lack of self-reflection. Or rather, he'd liked its result. Sticking his head in the sand had kept him away from his self-doubts and created an illusion of invincibility even he had come to believe.

Trouble was, having hard-asses as therapists wasn't quite as appealing as it had been.

This afternoon, when he'd left Roger Adams's office in a funk, he'd only thought of Joy. He'd tried to shrug off the need to see her, but in the end, he'd lost the fight. Telling himself he was nuts, he'd boarded a plane headed for the Albany airport, not JFK. Then he'd rented a car and hopped on the Northway.

He took a deep breath, caught the scent of her shampoo and tried to get a little closer by bringing her hips forward in the chair. Her body was so small compared to his, but the strength he drew from her was immense. She was like a balm, her hands deep in his hair as she smoothed the tension from his head and neck. He rubbed his cheek against her sternum, liking the feel of the soft knit turtleneck and the warm woman beneath.

"I went to see someone today," he said, figuring he had to explain himself. "A man I've known for years."

She made a soft noise, encouraging him without prying.

"He and his wife have been married for two decades. It was a great marriage, or at least I always thought so."

He paused, having trouble coming up with the right words. "They were friends with Cass and her husband, too."

Joy's hands went down to his shoulders, rubbing over his muscles in a circular motion.

God, if he could have crawled up inside of her, he would have.

He cleared his throat. "I've always thought marriage was a bad idea. My parents didn't have a healthy one, and the older I've become, the more I've seen in the way of ugly relationships. But this couple, they were in love. They were happy. They were the exception that proved the rule."

Gray pulled back a little and looked at Joy. They were so close, he could see each one of her eyelashes. The darker rim around her iris. The pale freckles that dusted her nose.

"Today, the man confirmed that he's been cheating on his wife. And the woman he picked is a reporter who's probably only been using him in hopes of getting information." Gray shook his head. "The guy threw out his marriage vows to get laid by someone who doesn't give a damn about him. I just don't get it, but you know what's worse? I'm not even sure he knows why he did what he did."

Staring into her face, he found himself wanting to say more. "This guy… He's been trying to find a way to talk to his wife. He's chewed himself raw about coming clean, not that I have any pity for him. She's going to be heartbroken when he tells her."

Joy leaned down and kissed him lightly on the forehead. "I'm sorry."

"Frankly, I wanted to hit him, I really did." Gray

shrugged. "But the really disturbing thing is, I don't think the whole mess would have bothered me as much before…"

"Before what?"

"You."

Her eyes flared.

"I—uh…" Feeling awkward, he moved back, bracing his palms on his knees and leaning into his shoulders. "Talking to this guy today reminded me why my lack of faith in marriage is justified. But instead of feeling vindicated, I got…depressed. Uh, hell. I don't know."

He felt like an idiot all of the sudden. A spastic, exposed idiot.

He was not used to talking about emotions, wasn't big into the whole sharing thing. Hell, he was the last man on the planet likely to be confused with a sensitive, New Age guy.

But here he was, babbling. On his knees, for God's sake.

He glanced up at Joy, feeling uneasy. Her legs were still spread wide open, her hands resting on her thighs. For some crazy reason, he wanted to go back to the warmth she offered so generously.

"Come here," she said softly, holding her arms up to him.

She didn't have to ask twice.

"Am I freaking you out?" he asked as he gathered her against him and dropped his head onto her shoulder.

"No. Why would you?"

He shrugged. "Not exactly pulling off the strong, manly thing right now, am I?"

"Do you have to be strong all the time?"

"In my world, the weak get eaten."

"Well, you're with me right now. And I like this. A lot." She buried her fingers into the hair at his nape. "I'm glad you came to me. And I'm sorry about your friends."

For a long while, they stayed close, the crackling fire the only thing making any sound in the room.

"Gray?"

"Hmm?"

"What happened with your parents?"

His first instinct was to keep quiet. The dark secrets of his family's dysfunction were buried good and deep and he liked them that way. Pulling out the mess was going to hurt and stuffing the crap back in wasn't going to feel any better.

But damn it, he found himself talking.

"My mother is a..." Somehow, the word *slut,* although accurate, seemed too crude in front of Joy. "She and my father wanted very different things out of marriage. They had a rough time being together."

"Is that why you've never married?"

"I don't know." Now that was a lie. "Uh, yeah... probably. I was in the middle of it a lot and I decided I would never, ever, be like them. Live like that. Put a child through that."

Gray shifted back and looked into her eyes. In a crystal-clear vision, he saw her as his wife. As the woman he woke up next to every morning. As the one individual on the face of the planet he could trust. As the person he went to for comfort and to whom he offered comfort in return.

"There are moments when I'm with you," he whispered, "that I forget everything I know is true. That I want to rely on things I know aren't safe."

Her lips parted in surprise.

Seeing her in the firelight, measuring the warmth in her eyes, he could sense something about to come out of his mouth. Something that petrified him.

Three little words.

A spear of panic went through his chest and triggered an acid burn that rose up from his belly into his throat.

Don't say it, he thought. Don't you dare say it. You're confused. Overwrought for no good reason. Suffering from weeks of sleep deprivation.

God, he needed to pull himself together before he made another cruel mistake. He wasn't in love with her. He couldn't be. He just wasn't that kind of a man.

Kissing her once on the lips, he got to his feet and went back to the fire.

"But enough of me," he said sharply as he palmed his glass. "What have you been up to?"

He watched her close up, her legs coming together, her arms linking around her waist. Her eyes were wide and a little worried when they met his, but she accepted the change of subject.

"I—uh, I've been working on the sketches…."

As she spoke, Gray rattled around in his own skin.

He shouldn't have come, he thought as he sipped some bourbon. Now they were both upset over nothing. And she deserved more than being whiplashed around by a man who didn't know his ass from third base when it came to his feelings.

He never should have come.

GRAY'S EXPRESSION WAS TOO impassive for Joy to read and his quick mood change was equally unfathomable.

While she filled the silence with meaningless details of daily life, she kept hoping he'd stop her rambling and take them back to where they'd just been.

"So how long are you up here for?" she asked.

"I have to leave tomorrow morning."

"Oh."

"And I should probably go to my house now. It's late, isn't it?" He checked his watch.

"Only nine. You could stay for dinner." She pushed her hair back. "Although I was just warming up some stew before you came. Nothing fancy."

"That's okay. I'm not hungry."

She crossed her legs and fell silent, not really surprised.

Dimly, she heard a rhythmic tapping sound and realized she was the one making it. Her foot was striking the leg of the table next to her like a metronome.

His eyes tracked the movement and then slowly slid up her calf, her knee, her thigh. His gaze settled on her breasts and his lids lowered, as if he wanted to hide what he was feeling from her.

"I think I'll go," he said quickly. As he turned to get his coat, she saw his body in profile against the fire. The evidence of his arousal was almost, but not completely, hidden in the folds of his fine slacks.

The urge to yell at him was nearly irresistible.

The man flies hundreds of miles out of his way to come and see her. He gives her a lovely, thoughtful gift. Tells her intimate, private things. And then waltzes out as though none of it was particularly significant.

"I hope you have a good week," he said casually as he slipped into his jacket. "I'll call you when I get back to the city. Maybe in the afternoon, more likely later in the evening."

As if she were just going to wait around to hear from him and he liked it that way.

Yeah, whatever.

She was suddenly damn tired of the go-away-come-closer game he was playing.

"I'll be out tomorrow night," she muttered.

His eyes flashed at her, his brows tightening. "And where are you going?"

She shrugged, getting to her feet with a burst of annoyance. "Nowhere important."

When she started to move past him, he took her arm.

"If it doesn't matter, then tell me."

As she measured his dark intensity, she wished she hadn't blurted out her plans. She had nothing to hide, but he wasn't going to like who she was having dinner with.

"Actually, I'm going out with Tom."

Gray dropped his hand.

"It's no big deal. His sister is coming to town—"

"I hope you enjoy yourself." He started to leave the room.

"Gray—Gray!" She grabbed his hand and was grateful when he stopped of his own accord. "Please, let's not end tonight like this."

He looked over his shoulder. His eyes were flat, lifeless. And harder to meet than when they'd been glacial.

"Don't worry about it. You and I never agreed on monogamy, did we? And just because I was your first, doesn't mean I'll be the last. In fact, that's one thing I can count on."

She gasped, stepping back. "I can't believe you just said that."

"Why? It's the truth." He dragged a hand through his hair. "You're young, beautiful, incredibly compassionate. And even though it kills me, I'm realistic enough to know that sooner or later you're going to find the right man for you."

"Gray, I haven't been with anyone else but you. I don't *want* to be with anyone else except you."

"You'll get over that," he said bitterly. "In fact, I want you to go out with Tom. It'll speed up the process. Put us both out of our misery."

Pain ripped through her.

As if the warmth she'd just given him was such a terrible burden?

Damn him.

"How dare you! How…" She couldn't think of anything else that covered what she was feeling. "How *dare* you! You think you're so experienced and sophisticated, but you know what? You're just jaded and cynical."

"All the more reason for you to move along."

She fell silent, just staring at him.

"You're right." She pushed her hair back with a slash of her hand. "I do need to end this because God knows you're pushing me right to the edge. After this little interlude with you, I'm dying to be with a man who makes some sense."

Gray closed his eyes and cursed. "This whole thing between us was wrong from the beginning and it's only gotten…more wrong. Look, you were absolutely right about that Tiffany's charade. I don't want to get married. I'm never *going* to get married. I had no business dragging you there and throwing rings at you, and I had no business coming after you tonight, either. I don't know what I'm doing here, I really don't. In fact, when I'm around you, I don't know what I'm doing at all."

"So maybe you should stop seeing me," she snapped. "Stop calling me. Leave me the hell alone. Because I don't need this kind of…relationship." She rolled her eyes. "God, I don't even know if that word fits us."

"I'm sorry. I never meant to hurt—"

"Shut up!" God, she felt like slapping him. She really did. "I don't want to hear another apology coming out of your—"

Joy fell silent.

A strange odor had suddenly permeated the room.

Gray must have noticed it, too, because he glanced over his shoulder, toward the dining room.

And then there was a loud *whoomp!* followed by a mighty shaking as an explosion rocked the mansion.

CHAPTER THIRTEEN

JOY SHOT OUT OF THE study, heading for the rear of the house where the noise had come from. The moment she entered the dining room, she stopped dead. In the kitchen, flames were alive and climbing the walls. Smoke poured out of the open double doors, bouncing along the ceiling. She felt the rush of heat on her face like a hot wind.

Gray hauled her back, shouting over the roaring sound, "We have to get out of the house!"

"My grandmother's upstairs!"

Gray pressed a cell phone into her palm and shoved her toward a door that opened to the outside.

"Call 9-1-1. I'll bring her down. Which bedroom?" he yelled.

Before she could answer, she realized with horror there was a shape moving among the flames. Her grandmother was in the kitchen.

"Grand-Em!" she screamed, lunging forward. "No!"

Gray caught her. "I'll get her! Use that phone!"

Joy was momentarily paralyzed by the sight of him disappearing into the fire. What snapped her mind into gear was the thought that he and Grand-Em might need to be treated for smoke inhalation. Or maybe something worse.

With her eyes watering from the stench and the heat,

she dialed quickly, giving her address and what she knew, which wasn't much. By now, the flames were licking out into the dining room, consuming the moldings along the ceiling, scorching the plaster. She backed up, but she couldn't leave. Not without Gray and Grand-Em.

Searching the flames and smoke, she heard a hissing sound, like steam or gas being released. And then a second explosion sent her flying back against the wall.

"Gray!"

She scrambled outside, tripping and flailing around before finding her footing and running toward the kitchen door. She skidded to a halt as she took in the spreading devastation. Violent orange tongues licked through the popped glass panes of the alcove's windows. Smoke billowed up into the cold night air in great, oily swells. The heat was so intense, it banished the night's chill.

He must be dead.

They both had to be dead.

Joy fell to her knees on the grass, taken down by a pain like nothing she'd ever felt before. Not even the loss of both her parents came close.

Through her sobs, she heard distant sirens and thought, *You're too late. You're too damned late. What was worth saving has already been lost.*

She felt something bite into her hand and looked down. Gray's cell phone.

She clutched it tighter and stared into the churning inferno.

Movement caught her eye. Over to the right.

From around the back of the house, a shadow lurched. No, it was a tall figure. Silhouetted against the shifting light of flames. A tall figure carrying something.

"Gray!" She leaped to her feet and ran without touching the ground. "Gray!"

His knees gave out just as she reached him and he sank to the grass, heaving great breaths into his lungs while gently laying Grand-Em out flat. The elderly woman was dazed and so was he. They were both covered in ash.

"Oh, Gray." Joy kissed his face. "How did you get out—"

"Through the office. I broke the window and—" A coughing fit overcame him and he couldn't seem to catch his breath.

"Here!" she called out as the fire truck and ambulance pulled up. "Over here!"

Paramedics came jogging to them as the firemen started pulling out hoses. Oxygen masks were quickly put on both Gray and Grand-Em and then the two of them were moved farther from the fire. While they were being worked on, Joy hovered around the knot of medics, knees loose at the near miss.

When she was sure neither was injured seriously, she looked over her shoulder. The rear portion of the house was consumed by flames.

How could it possibly—

A cold dread hit her. The stove. The burner. She'd left the burner on. But surely that wouldn't have caused such an explosion. Except what if after she'd fiddled with those dials, she'd left something else on?

Just as the thought occurred to her, Frankie's Honda came down the driveway.

"Frankie!" Joy called, a sob coming from her throat. "Oh, God…Frankie. Frankie!"

She rushed to her sister as Frankie slowly got out of the car. Nate came around from the passenger side with a similar shell-shocked expression.

Frankie's eyes were wide. "Joy… My God, are you all right?"

Joy was crying openly as she embraced her sister. "Yes, yes…Gray saved Grand-Em. But, oh Frankie, I think I did this. I think this is my fault—"

"Shh." Frankie cradled her while focusing on the fire. "You're hysterical. Let me go talk to the firemen."

THE BATTLE AGAINST THE blaze was still ongoing when the paramedics decided Grand-Em had to be taken to the Burlington Medical Center for observation. Joy volunteered to go along, but she didn't want to leave without talking to Gray and couldn't seem to find him in what was now a throng of people.

Two more fire trucks had come. Another ambulance. Two policemen. And all of the men seemed big and tall.

As Grand-Em was being loaded into the back of an ambulance, Joy frantically searched for Gray in the chaos.

"Ma'am? Excuse me, ma'am?" One of the paramedics put his face in front of her. "Ma'am, we have to go now. Are you coming?"

She tore her eyes away from the scene. "Yes," she said hoarsely. "But I need to—"

Suddenly, Gray materialized at her side. His suit was ruined, his hair coated in ash, his face streaked with black. She wanted to throw her arms around him and nearly did. What stopped her was the faraway look in his eyes as he spoke to her.

"Your sister, Nate and Spike will be staying at my house. Do you know the number?"

"Yes."

"And you'll stay there, too. For however long it takes to get White Caps back in livable shape. You're going with Emma to the hospital?" When she nodded, he asked, "How will you get home from Vermont?"

"Frankie will come get me tomorrow morning."

He nodded and looked away. "Okay. Take care of yourself."

"Is this goodbye?" she whispered.

"Ma'am, we've really got to go," the paramedic interrupted. "Do you need help getting in?"

She gave Gray another moment to respond. When he said nothing, she took the other man's hand and stepped up into the ambulance.

The paramedic got in with her and paused before shutting the double doors. He looked at Gray. "Don't worry, sir, we'll take good care of your wife and her grandmother."

As the doors were shut, Joy could have sworn she heard Gray say, "She's not my wife."

The engine flared and the ambulance jerked and Joy blinked back fresh tears. Staring out of the back window, she watched as Gray stood in the driveway, hands in his pockets, face in shadow.

THE NEXT MORNING Joy spent an hour walking around the hospital grounds. The sunshine was bright, though not particularly warm, and the chilly fresh air was just what she needed. After a night spent upright in a chair in her grandmother's room, she felt like she was packed in cotton wool.

Or maybe she was still in shock.

The guilt of knowing that the fire was her fault ate her alive. She'd endangered people's lives. Gray's. Grand-Em's. The firemen's. She'd burned part of the family's house down. Ruined her sister's wedding. Destroyed countless personal effects and family heirlooms.

And that wasn't the half of it.

Every time she closed her eyes, she saw Gray racing into the burning kitchen and she relived what it felt like to think he was dead. Then she pictured him telling her to take care of herself as if he were saying goodbye.

God, she felt as if she'd been punched in the chest.

Trying not to get sucked into her own head again, Joy looked up at the sun, noting the shift in its angle.

Frankie should be here by now, she thought dully.

She scanned the cars in the parking lot, looking for the Accord.

"There you are."

She wheeled around at the familiar, deep voice. "Gray?"

"I've been waiting in your grandmother's room and I just saw you from out of the window."

She searched his face, reassuring herself that he was well. And that he wasn't a figment of her imagination. "What are you doing here?"

"Your brother was released this morning ahead of schedule. Frankie had to go down to Albany and pick him up, and Nate had to start the fun and games with your insurance carrier. I volunteered to pick you up."

"Oh. That was awfully kind."

"How are you?" His eyes were shrewd. He knew, she suspected, that she was falling apart inside.

"I'm…"

The word she was searching for was *fine,* Joy told herself. She just needed to be strong and say it.

I'm fine, Gray. Thank you kindly for asking. I'm not a basket case who's going to come undone just because she torched her family's house and put her grandmother in a hospital bed and made the man she loved risk his life running into an inferno. Really, I'm just fine.

Fine.

"I'm…" She put her hand to her mouth and squeezed her eyes shut. She felt him reach for her, but pride and a fear of losing it completely made her step back. She was too raw not to rely on him for strength and unsure whether he'd honestly welcome the burden of her tears.

"No, no, I'm okay. Truly. I don't want you thinking I'm some kind of—"

"No offense, but shut up, Joy," he murmured, taking her into his arms.

She resisted him for, oh, maybe half a second. And then she collapsed into his body, wrapping her arms around his waist, holding on tight. He felt so good. So strong.

But she told herself she shouldn't read anything into the hug, that he was just offering compassion. He'd made his position clear right before the fire had broken out. No tragedy, no drama, was miraculously going to solve their problems. She forced herself to let go of him.

"So we, uh, we should probably go. But I'd like to say goodbye to Grand-Em." She turned and headed for the front doors.

His voice stopped her. "Frankie told me you think

you started the fire. But you should know the firemen believe the stove was faulty and that the gas connection in the back ruptured. It was probably a manufacturer's defect and the explosion was triggered by the pilot in the oven, not the burner you'd been using on the stove top."

She could only stare over her shoulder at him, picturing her hands twisting all those knobs. God only knew what she had turned on.

"Listen to me," he repeated. "It wasn't your fault."

"I guess it just feels that way."

And it was hard not to believe that their problems weren't because of her, too. If she were only a little more sophisticated, maybe they could have kept going. Enjoyed an exciting affair like a couple of grown-ups. Parted later, down the road, with affection.

She made herself get going and Gray followed her inside the hospital. After kissing her grandmother on her cheek, Joy and Gray walked out together. He led the way over to a nondescript rental sedan.

As they pulled away from the complex, she said, "You know, it just dawned on me. I don't know if I thanked you for what you did last night. You saved Grand-Em's life. At the risk of your own."

He shrugged. "There was no way I was going to let your grandmother die while you watched. Not when there was some way I could get to her."

They were silent until they reached the ferry that would take them back to New York State.

"I thought you had to return to the city," she said as they drove onto the boat's flat deck.

"I do. I'm heading down as soon as I drop you off at my house."

"Oh." She knitted her fingers together in her lap.

"It was generous of you to let my family stay with you last night. I promise we'll find somewhere else to live as soon as we can."

"The hell you will. And don't start. I've already had this argument with your sister. She didn't win it and neither will you. The house is empty and Libby loves taking care of people. You and your family will stay for however long it takes. Through the spring. I don't care."

As the ferry trudged across Lake Champlain, Joy looked out the car window at the water. The waves were dark and choppy, reflecting the fast-moving clouds overhead.

"Gray?" She glanced across at him. He was staring out the front windshield, at the opposite shore. His brows were together, his eyes unblinking.

"Yeah?"

"Am I ever going to see you again?" The question was out before she could stop it.

"Do you honestly want to?" he said softly.

Good question, she thought. And probably one she shouldn't answer, at least not out loud. Because what had really changed between them?

She opened her mouth anyway. "After I saw you go into that fire last night, and the second explosion hit, I was convinced you were dead. I couldn't breathe I hurt so much."

When he didn't answer, when his expression didn't change, she turned away.

There was a long pause and then she heard him shifting in his seat. "Here. Take this."

She looked back over to him. He was holding out a thin card. "What is it?"

"The key to my suite at the Waldorf. I talked with

Cassandra this morning. She's leaving for a couple of weeks so you won't be able to stay with her when you come down to the city. I want you to use my place. I'm going to be in Washington for most of the next month."

It was a logistical response, addressing nothing of what she'd been getting at, so she could only assume things really were over.

"That's very kind of you," she said stiffly, thinking there was no way in hell she was going to take him up on the offer. "But I can find—"

"You will stay with me when you're in the city. It's safer."

She frowned at his dictatorial tone. "Gray, I'm not your responsibility."

"I want to take care of you."

"Why? I'm operating under the assumption that we ended things last night."

He ignored the statement. "Two weeks from today I'm throwing a party in your honor at the Congress Club. Cass is contacting the fashion editors of *Women's Wear Daily*, *Vogue* and the *Times*. They'll all be coming. And she's going to try and get back to the city in time for it, as well."

Joy stared at him, dumbfounded. "Why are you—"

"I suggest you bring a number of your sketches so they can be posted in frames around the reception area. You will also address the crowd, so start thinking about your remarks. No more than six to eight minutes and I'll look them over for you before the event, if you like."

"Answer me, Gray," she said sharply. "Why are you doing this?"

"Because I want to help you."

"Why?"

"After the event, when you're written up in the three publications, you'll get a big response. You're going to need to hire an assistant and get a New York phone number, but the folks in my office will help set those up."

She shook her head. "I can't let you do this. I won't let you."

"I already have. All you need to do is show up."

"Which I'm not going to do." God, she was never going to understand the man. There was nothing between them, and he was planning all this for her?

"Don't be silly, Joy. Of course you'll be there."

"No. I. Won't."

In the long silence that followed, she thought perhaps that was the end of the conversation. But then he reached across the seat and took her hand.

"Do you know what kept me up last night?" His words seemed slow, rusty. As if he were forcing them. "After the flames were out, some of the firemen were walking around with flashlights. One of them stood in front of what was left of that stove and said he was surprised that no one was killed. I, uh, I pictured you, reheating that stew you were having, stirring a spoon in a pan. And I imagined what would have happened if I hadn't showed up. If we hadn't been talking in the study when the thing…"

His hand squeezed hers so hard she nearly cried out. But then he loosened his fingers and stroked her wrist.

"Look, I'm lousy at relationships, Joy, but I know all about positioning people for success. At least I can do right for you in one way." When she stayed silent, he rubbed his thumb over her palm. "Okay?"

"No, it really isn't. I feel like we're back where we

were, skating around each other, not really committed to anything. Tied together, but not really."

"Then just take me out of it and think in terms of your designs. You loved working with Cass, didn't you? And the result was fantastic. She said she was beating compliments off all night long at the Hall Gala. Now, you've got some other clients. You play this right and you could make a living doing what you love. This reception will help you get there."

She forced herself to get past her frustration. He was right in one respect. She did love working with the clients and making the gowns. And this kind of opportunity for a young designer starting out on her own was like winning the lottery.

But how could she let him do this?

"Joy?"

God, the girl in her wanted to turn him down because the whole thing was linked to Gray when she really wasn't. But the woman in her pointed out she'd be nuts to pass on the exposure.

"I just wish I understood you better," she said softly.

But then she thought, No, that's wrong. She understood him perfectly well. What she wished was that he could commit to her and to hell with her career plans.

"I want to do one thing right with you," he said. "Just one thing, I want to do right. I'd consider it a…favor, if you'd let me do this."

The rest of the trip back to his house was a quiet one. After he pulled up to the back door, he led her inside.

"I'll bet you want a shower and a lie-down," he said. "Let me show you where you'll sleep."

She followed him upstairs and down a corridor that

ran to the lake side of the house. At the end, he opened a door into a room that was done in black, cream and gold.

"You'll be staying in my room."

Her eyes immediately went to the bed.

"Don't worry, Libby changed the sheets."

When she heard the door shut, she turned around, thinking he'd left her.

But no. He was still in the room.

"Bath's through there," he said, nodding to a corner.

She looked over. "So it is."

There was a long silence. She frowned, thinking he had an odd expression on his face, one she couldn't quite read. He was staring at her, his big body very still.

"Forgive me," he said in a low voice.

"For what?"

"This."

He crossed the distance between them in two strides, took her face into his hands, and kissed her as though he *really* meant it.

Hard. Demanding. Deep.

After she got over the shock, she fell against his body, grabbing his back. Too soon, he was breaking the kiss and putting his head down on her shoulder.

"Joy..." He took a deep breath. "It kills me to think of you with another man, but I'm not going to curtail your life. I hope you see whoever you want to up here. Just know that I'll be thinking of you. Wanting you. And I hope when you're down in the city, we can... be together."

"Together how?"

He lifted his head and kissed her, burying his hands

in her hair. The force of his passion burned through her clothes, her skin, her heart.

"I keep thinking I'll be able to let you go," he murmured. "But I can't seem to do it."

Well, at least that was something she could understand. For all the reasons she needed to cut him loose, the idea of never seeing him again gave her the cold cringes.

But she just couldn't comprehend how he thought she'd be with anyone else.

"What's it going to take," she whispered, "for you to trust me?"

Gray shook his head. "I don't have to trust you."

"You're wrong about that."

"No, I'm not. I want you. That's enough."

After he left, she sat down on the bed, thinking she'd phrased it wrong. She needed to feel trusted if they were going to be together.

God, they were back where they started.

Nowhere. Except for the passion.

A COUPLE OF NIGHTS LATER, Joy woke up in a cold sweat, jolted from sleep by the bad dream that had been dogging her since she'd watched Gray go into the fire. In her nightmare, everything was just as it had happened that evening. The smells, the sights, the sounds. Except Gray didn't come back out of the house.

Shaky, overheated, she slid from his bed and padded over the Oriental rug to the bathroom. The marble floor of the bath was cold under her feet and the water she splashed on her face was so icy it numbed her cheeks.

There'd be no going back to sleep, at least not for a while, so she pulled on a black cashmere robe that smelled like Gray and went downstairs. When she got to the first floor, she saw a glow coming from the back of the house.

"Frankie?" she called out.

"No, Alex."

She walked into the kitchen. Her brother was warming something on the stove, wearing nothing but flannel pajama bottoms. One side of them had been ripped open to accommodate the cast and a couple of safety pins held the fabric together above his knee.

He must be cold, she thought, though she knew better than to suggest he put on more clothes.

"You hungry?" he said without looking up.

"No. Do you want help?"

"I think I can handle Campbell's chicken noodle by myself."

God, he was so thin now, she thought, easing herself into a chair at the table. Years of hard physical labor on sailboats had put pounds and pounds of muscle on his big frame and much of that was still with him. The difference was that any small layer of fat he'd had had been stripped from under his skin. His muscles were set in such stark relief, she could see their individual striations.

He took the pan from the stove, poured the steaming soup into a bowl, and then grabbed for his crutch. He carefully limped over to the table and spilled a little broth as he sat down. His face got fierce as he used his napkin to mop up.

He dunked his spoon, but he didn't bring any of the food to his lips. He just stirred.

"Not sleeping well?" he asked her.

"No."

"Nightmares?"

"How did you know?"

"Been there. Still doing that." His brows came together, as if he were forcing himself to focus. Slowly he lifted a spoonful up from the bowl. He blew on it and then put it into his mouth.

Joy let out a breath she wasn't aware she'd been holding.

The soft sound made Alex frown, as if he knew she was glad he was eating and he didn't appreciate her concern.

"It's not just the dreams," she said quickly. "I really can't sleep at all."

"You didn't burn down White Caps. You read the fire inspector's report."

"That's not what's keeping me up."

"So what is?"

"I watched the man I love go into a flaming room. It's not something I'm going to forget."

Alex's eyes snapped up to hers. "So you've got it that bad for Bennett?"

"Yes. But don't tell Frankie. Don't tell…anyone."

He shook his head. "Watch yourself, Joy."

"I know. He's a lady killer. I've heard it all before. I tell it to myself."

"Doesn't help, does it?"

"What?"

"Telling yourself what to feel." He went back to his soup.

"No, it doesn't." She watched as he ate some more, wondering about his private life. It was odd to know so little about the brother she loved so much. "Have you ever been in love, Alex?"

"Yes."

Now that surprised her. "Really?"

He nodded.

"What happened?"

"Nothing good. That's why I'm telling you to watch yourself. Even if Gray Bennett was a model of monogamy, and he isn't, love is one long, rough road. To be avoided if possible."

"Who was she?"

But Alex was finished talking. She could tell by the way his mouth had flattened. The closing down, shutting off, reminded her of Gray.

God, maybe the two of them should go out together. They'd be so damned comfortable in each other's oppressive silences, reveling in the utter lack of intimacy.

"So when are you heading back to the city?" Alex asked.

"Now that Frankie and Nate aren't having a big wedding, I guess I'll go down sooner. And with Libby agreeing to watch Grand-Em, I feel a little more free about leaving."

"Are you going to stay with Cassandra?"

She narrowed her eyes. His tone was so casual, too casual. Especially in light of the tension that had lifted his shoulders and made him grip his spoon as though it might slip out of his hand.

"Is it her?" Joy asked quietly. "Is she the one you loved?"

"No."

"I think you're lying."

Alex lifted the spoon to his mouth. He paused, staring down at the bowl. "Doesn't matter if I am."

"Damn it, it matters to me," she snapped.

Alex's eyes shot across the table.

Before he could say anything, she linked her arms over her chest and glared at him. "Why the hell am I so untrustworthy? Will you please tell me? I mean, do I give off some kind of disreputable vibe? Because I just don't get it."

Her brother slowly put the spoon down. "Who said you were untrustworthy?"

"You are, right now. What do you think I'm going to do? Race up to Cassandra and spill your secret?"

"No," he said slowly. "You won't do that because I don't have a secret to tell."

"Oh, right. It couldn't possibly have anything to do with the fact that I have some integrity." She got up. "My mistake."

He grabbed her hand. "What the hell's going on, Joy?"

"Nothing. Nothing is going on. Absolutely *nothing* is going on."

"Sit down."

"I don't feel like it. Now let go of me." She wrenched free of his grip and went over to a window. Outside, the full moon gleamed in a cloudless, cold sky.

"Yes. I love her."

Joy wheeled around.

Alex wasn't looking in her direction at all. And he seemed to have retracted into himself, his big body more compact than usual.

"Alex…"

"I started loving her the moment I first saw her run into my best friend's arms. It's been a hellacious six years and now that Reese is…gone, there's no end in sight." His vivid blue eyes flashed up at her. "I don't like admitting this to myself. It's got nothing to do with trusting you."

Joy went back to the table. "Does she know?"

He shook his head. "Only you and God do. And it has to stay that way. Do we understand each other?"

She nodded, sinking down into a chair. "Perfectly."

In the silence that followed, she watched as he ate.

"So I'm leaving soon," he said abruptly.

"Going where?" She tried to keep her alarm to herself.

"There's a bathroom with a shower in Dad's old workshop. I figure I can move a bed in to the space."

"But the shop's not heated."

"There's a potbellied stove. I'll be okay." He fiddled with the spoon, running it in circles through the soup. "There are too many people in this house. And I don't like living off Bennett's hospitality."

"Have you told Frankie?"

"Yeah. She blew a gasket, but she knows she can't stop me. I did promise to stay here until my next check-up with the ortho doc. But then I'm gone."

A feeling of unease curled around Joy's heart. "Alex, if you slowly kill yourself, I will never forgive you."

He smiled coldly into his soup. "Trust me, if I wanted to be dead, I'd be in the ground already. I've always known where the shotgun was in the house."

CHAPTER FOURTEEN

THE FOLLOWING WEEKEND, Joy watched Frankie and Nate get married in the county courthouse. Spike was the other witness. Frankie wore a tailored pantsuit because the gown Joy had worked so hard on had been ruined by smoke and water. Nate was in a jacket and tie.

Seeing her sister dressed as if she were going to a job interview instead of taking a husband made Joy want to cry for everything Frankie had missed out on. The dress. The veil. The big party.

But the funny thing was, Frankie and Nate didn't seem to mind the change in clothes or venue or plans. Heck, they didn't even seem to notice they weren't in a cathedral when the judge addressed them in his chambers. The two of them were glowing like stars, especially as they shared their first kiss as husband and wife.

Joy, on the other hand, felt the losses acutely. Especially as she signed the papers as a witness. It just didn't seem fair, and manufacturer's defect or not, she still blamed herself for the fire.

Following a quiet dinner at a local, 1950s era dive called the Silver Diner, the four of them went back to Gray's house. They'd just walked in the door when Libby called down the back stairs from her room.

"Joy, is that you?"

"Hi, Libby," she answered. "It's me. All of us, actually."

There was a scamper of dog feet and then Ernest shot down the stairwell. He did a quick meet-and-greet of the assembled bipeds while his owner came into the kitchen. Libby was wearing a pink fuzzy bathrobe and slippers and her white hair was matted on one side, as if she'd been reading in bed.

The woman smiled at Joy. "You just missed young Mr. Gray's call. He said he was traveling, but that he might try you later."

"Oh. Thank you."

In the past week, Gray still phoned her as much as he had before, but now she saw his actions in a different light. Did he time the calls early in the morning and late at night not because he was busy, but because he was checking up on her? And did he ask her about her day because he was trying to ferret out whether or not she'd been dating someone?

He'd told her he didn't care what she did up north, but she wasn't sure she believed him.

Which made them equal, she supposed. Because he didn't believe in her, either.

Frustration crept into her chest, making her lungs burn. The sensation was so familiar to her by now that she barely noticed it.

"So where have you all been?" Libby asked, as if they were children coming in from a night of fun. "You left before I got back from my brother's."

"We were getting married," Frankie said. She flashed

a simple gold band and a dazzling smile while her new husband nuzzled her neck.

"Why didn't you say something!"

Libby rushed forward to embrace the couple and Ernest, ever ready for a group hug, planted his forepaws on Nate's hip.

"With everything that's been going on, we just wanted to keep it quiet," Frankie said.

"Shall I get out the champagne?"

Frankie looked at Nate and smiled. "That would be great."

The five of them split a bottle while sitting around the kitchen table. As Joy watched her sister and Nate, she felt as though her heart were going to break. She was reminded of when she'd seen them together in this very same room, on the night of Gray's father's birthday party. She'd been struck by the depth of their love and the shallowness of her own daydreams.

Now, the comparison between what they had and what was going on with Gray was even harder to bear.

Later, she went up to his bedroom, took a shower and slid between the sheets. She was lying on her stomach, one of his pillows tucked against her body, when the phone rang on the bedside table. Instinctively she reached for it, but then figured it was probably Gray's private line as the phone out in the hall wasn't ringing, as well.

She wondered who was on the other end and decided she'd rather not know. Ever since the conversation with Alex, she'd been thinking about what Gray was doing down in Washington. He'd said he didn't care who she saw up north so it wasn't unreasonable to wonder whether he was with other women down south.

And wasn't that a great thought to try and fall asleep on.

After four rings, the phone fell silent.

GRAY FLIPPED HIS CELL phone shut and did not look at his watch. He knew damn well it was after midnight.

Joy was either not answering his phone. Or she still wasn't home.

Why in the hell had he told her he didn't care who she saw up north?

He cared. He cared deeply. He cared until he couldn't think of anything but her. Until all he knew was that he missed her and he felt...well, something close to unclothed without her by his side.

Exhausted, Gray rubbed his eyes and wished he were not at yet another Washington party. Through the door he'd shut for privacy, the churning, relentless noise of people drinking and talking and laughing seeped into the parlor. John Beckin threw a mean shindig, he always had, but tonight Gray was not in the mood.

Putting off the inevitable, he wandered around, looking at the trinkets and the paintings and the photographs.

He kept hearing Joy's voice in his head.

What's it going to take for you to trust me?

I don't need to trust you.

His response had been honest, but maybe all wrong. First of all, if it were true, he wouldn't feel so wretched right now. And second, where did that leave her? Wouldn't she need to feel that he had some faith in her?

What's it going to take for you to trust me?

God, he feared that question, he really did. Because the more time he spent with her, the more attached he got and the harder it was to let go of his past. It was getting damn near impossible to put aside images of his father looking broken.

And he kept hearing the sounds of doors opening and closing as his mother's lovers left.

Damn it, he knew Joy was not his mother. But he also knew that she'd just had her first lover. Sort of. And that she was entering the New York City arena after having been cloistered upstate all her life. She was a stunning beauty with a good heart. Didn't she deserve to be free to explore?

Gray rubbed the center of his chest. Explore?

Oh, come *on,* Bennett. Like the dating scene in Manhattan was a flipping National Geographic special?

Well, there were a lot of animals in the Big Apple.

Yeah, and if one of them so much as shook her hand, Gray was going to go commando. He wanted her as his own and no one else's.

So where did that leave them?

The answer was easy. And shattering. He probably should just step up to the plate and tell her that he wanted them to be together. Exclusively. As in boyfriend and girlfriend, though the words seemed ridiculous considering they were both adults.

Except as he contemplated coming forward with that little proposal, all he felt was a cold void. The sensation reminded him of what had been bouncing around in his body when he'd almost blurted out that *I love you* the night of the fire.

He massaged his sternum again. Ah, hell, he was afraid.

But why?

Because maybe, just maybe, he thought, the root of the problem wasn't in his past or her present. Maybe it had nothing to do with time. It was entirely possible that he was just a coward who didn't want to get his heart broken.

Gray winced.

Damn, no wonder he tried to avoid thinking about his feelings. Self-actualization was about as much fun as getting a thigh bone set.

The thoughts about boyfriends and girlfriends made Gray pause by a black-and-white photograph of a group of college kids. A young John Beckin, his deceased wife, Mary, and what must have been their cronies, were sitting in football bleachers wearing Yale sweatshirts.

God, Becks seemed so young, but his intensity was already shining through. In the picture, he was looking over his shoulder. Staring, actually. With total absorption.

Gray frowned and bent down closer to the frame. Good Lord. Allison and Roger Adams were behind Becks.

And Allison was the one Becks was staring at.

Gray picked up the picture.

The woman didn't seem to be aware of the attention. She was looking at her future husband, laughing at something Roger had said, totally oblivious to the young man in front who was regarding her with…love.

A terrible feeling came over Gray, the same kind of nasty ache he'd had when his mother had used him.

"There you are," came a voice from across the room.

Gray turned, photograph still in hand. Becks was smiling as he walked into the parlor.

"We were worried you'd left, Bennett."

"You want her still," Gray said softly.

Becks seemed confused. "I'm sorry?"

"Allison Adams. You wanted her then." He turned the frame around. "You want her still. That's why you asked me to dig into the affair. You wanted to make sure she knew about the adultery and were betting that I'd force her husband to tell her or I'd go to her myself with what I found out. It had nothing to do with the leaks or the reporter or the Senate, did it?"

Becks looked down once before lying. "Don't be absurd, Gray."

"You know I'm tight with her. That I respect her. That I wouldn't feel right about keeping that kind of thing a secret." Gray shook his head and put the picture back. "You played me very well, Becks. Very, very well."

Becks's eyes were shrewd as he seemed to be assessing whether to keep lying or not. "Did you go to him?"

"Yes, I did."

"What did he say? Did he admit to it?"

"I'm not going to go into that with you. But he did assure me the leaks weren't from him, and I believe Roger." Partially on account of the fact that the senator had been crying at the time, but mostly because having an affair with a reporter was dangerous enough. Sharing secrets with a journalist you were laying was guaranteed career suicide and Roger Adams was smart enough to know that.

"She married the wrong man, Gray."

"That's your opinion."

"At least I never would have screwed around on her."

Gray shook his head, feeling himself go completely numb. "If you'll excuse me, I'm going to take off."

Becks reached out. "Gray, he cheated on her in college. He doesn't deserve her. He never did."

"And you do? You set me up to do your dirty work. I don't find a lot of integrity in that, but maybe I'm missing something."

Gray strode across the room.

Becks's voice was hard when he spoke. "We're not going to have any trouble between us, are we? Because that would be most unfortunate. I would hate to see you cut out of the profession you love so much."

Gray glanced over his shoulder.

The first rule of war was simple, he thought. When attacked, strike back mortally. A half-dead opponent is still perfectly capable of taking you out.

He turned around and pegged the other man with a flat stare.

"Do you really want to go there, Becks? Because I have enough information on you to sink you like a stone and I'm not at all sentimental. Just because you clerked for my father a million years ago doesn't mean I won't slaughter you where you stand." He took out his cell phone, casually tossing it up into the air and catching it. Over and over again. "To keep my job, I don't need thousands of voters to think I'm a nice, trustworthy guy, but you sure as hell do. Iran-Contra. The Senate check-writing scandal. Working the back channels on budget discussions. I know every dirty deed you've ever done and you want to know what should scare you even more? I have a file on you. Stuffed up good and thick with documents you've signed, memos you've written, pictures, too. One call to a newspaper and a couple of faxes and I can shatter that image you've spent a lifetime building. Oh, and did I mention, I have the *Washington Post* on speed dial? *New York Times,* too."

Becks went dead still, his pallor changing to a pearly gray. But he rallied soon enough, that famous engaging smile coming out. "Listen to us, we're not enemies. What are we carrying on about? I'm sorry that I put you in such a terrible position."

"So am I. But we're past apologies, Beckin. You've pissed me off so badly, I just might make those calls anyway. Someone with your standards shouldn't be at the head of the Senate and I suddenly despise myself for letting your conniving ass sully that seat for so long."

He opened the door and marched out of the room.

"Gray!"

With Becks on his heels, Gray strode out of the town house, signaled for his car and walked into the street. He was physically ill. Sick with himself. With Beckin. With Washington.

"Gray!" Becks grabbed his arm. "I can't let you go like this. We need to—"

"Think about retiring, Beckin, and do it soon. It'll be better than getting thrown out in the street by your peers."

"You wouldn't dare."

"You know my reputation. I don't aim unless I'm prepared to pull the trigger. Do yourself a favor and retire." He got into the limousine and told the driver to hit the gas.

"We going back to your place, boss?" his driver asked.

"No. Take me by the White House."

"Whatever you say, boss."

Two blocks before 1600 Pennsylvania Avenue, the Lincoln Town Car slowed at a stoplight.

"We going in the side entrance?" the chauffeur asked.

"No, just drive by it."

"Okay."

Up ahead, Gray could see the spotlit black iron fence and the green stretch of lawn. And then the White House rose like a beacon.

"Slow down," he said. "Actually, stop."

The driver brought the Lincoln to a halt.

Gray opened the door, stepped out and leaned back against the car. He stared at the building, remembering the first time he'd seen it. He'd been five years old and utterly convinced that something magical was happening inside.

There was still magic going on, he supposed. He just couldn't see it anymore. His intimate knowledge of Capitol Hill clouded his vision too much.

JOY FROZE IN THE PROCESS of packing her suitcase. The phone was ringing out in the hall. She held her breath, hoping that Libby's voice would carry up the stairs and tell her Gray was on the phone.

She'd missed each time he'd called in the last two days. Twice because she was helping clean up at White Caps. Once when she was having dinner with Frankie and Nate. And the last because she'd gone for a long walk to clear her mind.

She was due in New York this afternoon and wanted to see if he was going to be in town. After having done some research on hotels in Manhattan, the idea of saving hundreds of dollars by taking advantage of his hospitality was attractive. But she wanted to confirm that he'd be in Washington before she made her decision. Staying in close quarters with him seemed like torture.

She waited to hear Libby call out. There was nothing.

She closed her eyes and then resumed packing.

"Joy! It's Gray for you."

She walked quickly to the hall phone. "Gray?"

"Hi."

"I'm coming to town."

"When?" His voice was distant, but it could have just been because he was on his cell phone.

"Today. This afternoon."

"Well, my offer still stands. I'm in Washington, but you're welcome to stay at the suite."

"Thanks." She cleared her throat. "I appreciate it. God, everything in New York is so expensive."

"And don't be shy about ordering room service. Just put everything on my bill."

Yeah, not bloody likely. She wasn't about to mooch off him for food. "That's generous, but I can pay for my own meals."

"I'm busy down here, but I'll try to get away."

"Don't worry if you can't. I understand. So the elections are getting close, aren't they?"

"Yes. Listen, everything's set for your party."

Good Lord, how could she have forgotten about that? It was…five days away. At the end of this week.

"Joy? You still there?"

"Yes. Yes, I am."

"My assistant in New York will leave details at the suite for you and you'll be happy to know that Cassandra can't stand not being a part of it so she's cutting her vacation short to get back. I took the liberty of drafting some talking points for you. My assistant will get them to you. And you should wear something of your own design, something bright. You need to stand out in the crowd so people can find you. Also, I've had a trunk line installed in my office in the city. My assistant will handle any calls for you there and business cards have been printed with the number on it."

A chill went through her. "You have everything arranged, don't you?"

"I know how important this is going to be for your career." There was a pause and then she heard a commotion in the background, as if people were arguing. "Sorry, I've got to run. Take care, Joy, and have a safe trip."

The phone went dead.

She hung up the receiver and thought about what his friend the investment banker had said. That Gray was a makeup artist. That he turned people into whoever they had to be to get elected.

Looks as if she was just one more quick fix in a long line of them.

When she resumed packing, her hands were shaky. She told herself she was getting just what she wanted. A free place to stay in New York. A party to help launch her career. Him in Washington.

It was all good.

Except she did want to see him. Even if it was stupid. Even if they were going nowhere.

She thought back to that one night they'd spent together. Of that one moment when they'd been joined. Heat pooled in her belly.

Her heart wanted him. So did her body. Her mind was the only holdout, the only part of her that was making any sense.

So thank God for higher reasoning.

CHAPTER FIFTEEN

New York City in the rain was a nightmare, Joy thought as she slipped the card into the suite's lock. When the little green light flashed and she heard a metallic shift, she turned the brass handle.

The moment she was inside, she stepped out of her high heels and curled her damp, chilly feet into the thick carpet. She didn't turn on any lights. Anxious, irritated and wired, she needed to avoid stimulation as much as she could. Calming herself down so she'd be able to fall asleep was going to take some doing.

Picking up her shoes, she walked into her bedroom using the city's glow to find her way around. She peeled off her drenched raincoat and had to hang it up in the shower it was so soaked.

The weather had been gruesome and enduring, a cold, wet and windy rush since the moment she'd left the Waldorf that morning. And courtesy of the storm, she had yet another thing to add to her collection of New York City knowledge: getting a taxi in Manhattan when it was cold, wet and windy was like winning the lottery. She figured it would be sometime next summer before she thawed out.

What a day. She'd met with Cassandra's friends, separately. Had lunched with two more potential clients. And then, with what little time there had been left during business hours, she'd haggled over silk and taffeta in the garment district. The marathon had ended on a dinner with Cass. With the reception only two days away, they'd talked about who was coming and decided which of the sketches should be displayed.

Now, it was close to ten o'clock at night.

Not that she would have known it without a watch. She couldn't decide whether she thought it was actually four in the morning or high noon. Her internal engine was racing so out of control, she felt as if her body was two feet behind her brain.

What she needed was a bath. A long, hot bath.

She stuck her head out into the living room and eyed the open door to the bedroom Gray used. In his bath, she knew there was a Jacuzzi the size of a small pond.

For the past three days, she'd avoided his private space, but now she walked over to it. As soon as she stepped through the door, she didn't know why she'd bothered to keep out of the room. There was nothing of him in it. No personal effects, no papers. Just some clothes in the closet.

Her feet stopped in front of the bed of their own accord and she stared at the precisely arranged pillows. The fancy satin duvet. The matching padded headboard.

She couldn't imagine them ever getting back in the thing. Or any other bed.

Had they actually lain on it together in the first place?

Joy forced herself to go into the bathroom. The tub was located in a walled-off marble alcove, and as she measured its wide belly, she thought it could easily accommodate three people. Filling up the Jacuzzi was going to take some time so she cranked on the faucets and went back to her room where she changed and pulled on a robe.

Twenty minutes later she was in heaven. Settling into the water was like being hugged and her body sagged in the comfort. She reached out for a bath towel, folded it up into a thick square and put it behind her head as a cushion. Then she hit the jets.

That ruined the moment. The noise of rushing water and the currents against her skin were agitating. Silencing the Jacuzzi, she waited for the hot water to still and then closed her eyes.

GRAY STOOD OUTSIDE the door to the suite, frozen in place. He didn't know what he was going to find when he went inside.

In his mind, he saw his teenage self hesitating at his mother's bedroom. There was a piece of paper in his hand. On it, in big letters, was a message he'd written. His father had called and was coming home early. ETA was twenty minutes.

Through the closed door, he'd been able to hear the sound of a bed creaking softly.

That time, as with so many others, he'd knocked once and slipped the note inside. It was a code they'd developed and he hadn't waited for a response. Watching the men leave, all red-faced and disheveled, had always disgusted him.

He'd tried so hard to keep his mother's secrets, fearing that he would lose both his parents if he wasn't careful enough. He'd been convinced if they ever split, his father would be lost to his books and his judicial bench, and his mother would go off with her lovers, and then Gray would be alone. Nightmares about being left behind in dark, public places where strangers were cruel had plagued him for years.

The dysfunction, the treachery, the lying had seemed a small price to pay to avoid making his disturbing dreams a reality.

And hadn't all that training in deception been put to good use? His career in politics was based on everything he'd learned about hiding emotions, shading the truth, thinking ahead so you didn't get caught with your ass in the breeze.

The suspicion had seemed so natural. Until he'd been with Joy.

Forcing himself to slide the pass card into the lock, he opened the door slowly. Silence. Only silence.

No foreplay giggles or eager sighs. No grunts of a man getting off.

He let out his breath and wondered if maybe Joy hadn't come to town at all. He'd been unable to reach her at the suite, because she didn't know how to get the messages off the phone, or she hadn't wanted to return the ones he'd left.

Then again, it was only ten-thirty. She might still be out.

Unable to help himself, he went over to the second bedroom. There was a hair brush on the bureau. A scarf on the back of a chair. On top of the bed, there was a neatly folded skirt and a silk shirt.

Probably the clothes she'd worn during the day and had changed out of before going to dinner somewhere.

He walked to his own room, putting down his travel bag and peeling his suit jacket off. He let the thing fall to the bed and removed his tie and cuff links while kicking off his shoes. He wanted a shower. He wanted some food. He wanted a drink.

But he wanted Joy most of all.

God, he just wanted to go back to the moment when she'd held him against her body. When he'd babbled about disillusions and she hadn't scorned him for not being the tough guy he should be.

He undid his belt and dropped his trousers. Took off his boxers and socks.

His body was tight from travel and stress and sexual deprivation. As he stretched his arms over head, his back cracked and his skin ached.

A shower. Start with the shower, he thought. And while you're at it, try to ignore the fact that you're waiting for Joy to burst into this suite with Charles Wilshire. Or some other man.

Gray pushed the door to the bathroom open and frowned. The overhead lights were on dimly. There was a bathrobe thrown casually across the sink. And the air was warm. Moist.

Moving slowly, breath caught in his throat, Gray peered around into the alcove.

Joy was asleep in the Jacuzzi, her long, lithe body stretched out in the water. Her neck was arched, her head back on a towel, her hair flowing in strawberry-blond waves across the creamy marble. The tips of her breasts were just breaching the top of the water level, and with every slow, even breath she took, the rosy peaks popped out and glistened in the dim light. As she exhaled, they sank beneath the surface.

He stepped forward, drawn by her.

At the same moment, her lashes fluttered open and her sleepy gaze slid over to him.

"Gray!" As if she forgot she was naked, she sat up, one of her legs bending to give her leverage. The sight of the water sluicing down her pale breasts jolted him, but that wasn't the worst of it. Through the undulating surface of the bath, her core was revealed and hidden by turns.

And then her eyes latched on to his body.

Her lips parted as she watched his erection go rock-hard. He couldn't be sure whether she was horrified at his undisciplined reaction or hungry for him.

Hell, maybe it was his size. He was a big man, big all over. Maybe she was surprised at what had fit inside of her.

He knew he should grab a towel and cover up. He knew he should make some casual comment to put her at ease. He knew he should leave.

He could do nothing of the sort. He barely had the will to stay standing.

"Joy..." he breathed.

It was a question. And as good as he could do considering he could hardly speak at all.

Her eyes widened, as if she knew what he was asking for.

Her answer was to reach out her hand to him.

He closed his eyes at her trust. He'd done so little to deserve it, in his actions and his words and the thoughts he'd kept to himself. How in the hell could he ever have thought she'd be banging some random guy in his suite?

God, the lessons he'd learned from his mother were too good. Too ingrained. If the past could make him doubt someone like Joy, he was too broken ever to be fixed.

When he looked at her again, she'd dropped her hand

on the edge of the tub and was staring straight ahead. As if trying to figure out how she could get to her robe without going past him. The hurt on her face made him wince.

As he put one foot into the warm, soothing water, she glanced up in surprise.

Sinking down on to his knees, the size of him displaced gallons of water, kicking the stuff out over the gunnels of the tub and on to the floor. He didn't even hear the splashing. He was reaching through the gentle water for her body, bringing her close against him, wrapping his arms around her.

She was so soft, flowing over his skin and his bones, until he was convinced it was her, and not the bath, that warmed him. He kissed the first part of her that hit his mouth. Her neck. And then he worked his way up to her earlobe, nipping gently at the tender skin.

"Joy..." Her name left him on a sigh. "How I've missed you."

His hand swept down her spine and brought her lower body in full contact with him. His arousal folded up between their bellies, pushing against her soft skin. He was desperate. Insatiable. But very, very willing to wait.

As he rolled her over on top of him, the water rising up and soaking into his hair, he framed her face with his hands. He wrapped his legs around hers, holding her down against his body when she would have floated up.

"Slow," he said, before he kissed her. "This time, it will be slow. This time, I'll do right by you."

He slipped his tongue into her mouth and was rewarded by a return caress that sent his senses reeling.

She kissed him back with a hunger that nearly undid him, her hands grabbing onto his biceps and squeezing.

When he released her mouth, he loosened his hold on her legs and gently urged her up so she was straddling him. Her nipples were tight from passion and the chill of being free of the bath and he sat up, licking droplets of water from them. Taking one of the buds into his mouth, he stroked his tongue over the taut flesh and then flicked her quick once, twice, many times. As she gasped, he changed the loving, suckling her tenderly.

He pulled away, wanting to see her. Her head was tilted back, her hair trailing over her shoulders and down into the water. Her breasts were full, the nipple he'd had in his mouth reddened from his attentions. He went to work on the other one.

Her hands dove into his hair and he relished the way she was dragging him closer still to her breast. It was as if she couldn't get him near enough and he knew exactly how she felt.

They stayed in the bath for a long time, kissing and touching, but there were things he wanted to do to her that the water made impossible. So in one giant, messy motion, he lifted her out of the tub and carried her from the alcove. He held her against him, kissing her, as he reached over and grabbed a towel. He started drying her at her neck and moved down to her shoulders. As he blotted her breasts, he kissed them both and then worked his way down her taut stomach and her graceful hip bones.

The juncture of her thighs enthralled him, but he dropped to his knees and dried her feet and then her ankles. Moving up her calves, he rubbed her gently with the soft towel and then kissed her skin. When he got up to her thighs, he slowed.

Her breath was ragged, her eyes shimmering with heat as she stared down at him. He kissed her outer thigh. And then licked a small, pale mole. He tested her flesh with his teeth ever so delicately.

And then he ran the towel up the inside of her legs. He didn't want to rush her. In spite of the pounding lust in him, he waited to see if she would open herself to him.

Her weight shifted. Her thighs parted a little more.

JOY SWALLOWED THROUGH a dry throat.

Seeing Gray's dark head at her thighs, his long, elegant fingers working a towel over her skin, was nearly all she could handle. But she wanted him to touch her even more intimately.

Especially as his tongue came out and he licked that mole again.

He shifted, his head coming higher and moving in between her legs. She widened her stance a little further.

His hair was soft on her inner thigh.

"I want to be in your heat," he said against her skin. "Is that okay?"

"Oh, yes…."

There was a low grumble of satisfaction and then his hand urged her legs apart a little more.

But it was his mouth that made contact where she ached, not his fingers.

"Gray!" Lightning ripped through her, snapping her spine into a straight line.

He nuzzled her, pleasured her, his lips and tongue

hot and slow and delicious. She watched him when she could, amazed that this big, aroused man was on his knees before her, adoring her body as he was.

And adoring was the right word because his expression was one of pure bliss. As if he were getting as much out of the experience as she was.

When her knees gave out, he caught her easily.

"I'm not finished," he said, carrying her to the bed. "Not by a long shot."

He laid her down and went right back to where he had been. Her body was transformed by his loving, a bloom of heat starting where he was kissing her so thoroughly and spreading through every part of her.

And then without warning, he changed his tempo, speeding up, intensifying the caresses. She jerked under his mouth and thrashed her legs around until one flopped over his back. And then the world exploded and she called out his name, her breath stopping, her heart stopping, her thoughts stopping. She dissolved away, and when she condensed once more, he was lying beside her, nuzzling her neck, his tender words praising her.

Blindly, she turned onto her side and moved her body against his. His breath went in on a rasp when her stomach rubbed over his erection.

"I don't want to stop," she said. "I want more."

He laughed, a deep, masculine purr. "And I'm happy to oblige."

He rolled her onto her back and kissed her breasts, starting to move down her body again.

"No." She stopped him. Pulled him back up. "I want you…inside."

His eyes closed, his face tightening. "Joy, we don't have to."

"You're so hard, I can feel the beat of your heart on my hip."

Gray's lips peeled off his teeth as if her words excited him to desperation. "I'll be fine. Hell, I deserve this."

"No, you don't. Make love with me," she whispered, stroking his back. "Make love with me until we don't know which part of us is you and which is me."

His eyes flipped open. He gently stroked her face. "Are you sure?"

She nodded, capturing his nape, urging his mouth down. He kissed her long and slow, and when he pulled back, she heard the sound of that drawer opening. Through heavy lids, she watched as he sheathed his length, wondering how he was going to fit inside of her, reminding herself that he had once before.

Parting her thighs with his knee, he settled his weight on top of her, propping his shoulders and chest up with his elbows. Stroking her hair back, he kissed her forehead, then her temple, then her cheek. Her body moved under him of its own accord, straining, trying to get close.

One of his hands disappeared between them. His weight shifted and she felt him positioning himself against her.

And then in a slow, sweet movement, he pressed inside, stretching her, filling her. There was no pain. Just an incredible rush of pleasure.

His head dropped down to her shoulder as his body started to tremble.

"Does it hurt?" he asked thickly.

She was so busy absorbing the sensation, she barely heard him.

"Joy? I need to know. Should I pull out?"

"Oh, God, no…don't ever."

He seemed to relax a little. And then he started to move.

Joy arched against him, grabbing onto his hips. He was a sensuous, heavy tide rolling on top of her, inside of her, the friction of his body creating a growing heat. She threw her knees out as wide as they could go so she could have even more of him.

"That's right," he said, his guttural voice almost foreign. "Sweet woman, you're going to be the death of me."

His rhythm grew more powerful, though she sensed he was still holding back by the sweat that broke out over his skin, by the tense muscles that were churning against her.

"More," she demanded, nipping at his shoulder with her teeth. "Gray, give me more."

"Wrap your legs around my hips."

She did as he asked and gasped at the depths he hit as he surged forward, pulled away, came back. She sensed that there was something coming for her again, something he could share in if he let himself go, and urgency made her frantic.

"Don't hold back," she said, scoring his skin with her nails. "Come with me, Gray. Be free."

With a throttled growl, he slipped the chain on his control and give her everything he had, pumping into her hard and deep until she cried out his name and went rigid under him. From a great distance, she heard a wild roar and realized dimly that the sound had come out of his throat, out of his chest, maybe out of his soul. His body convulsed into hers again and again.

And then there was only stillness and their panting breaths.

When he started to roll off her, she complained the only way she could—by holding onto him.

"We have to be safe," he said with a voice gone straight to gravel. She felt his hand come between them and then he slid out of her body. "Even though I want to stay inside of you until I'm hard enough to do that again."

He settled her into his arms. And then he kissed her lips.

"I've never been so…wild before," he said softly. There was real wonder in his ragged voice. "Did I hurt you?"

She cozied up to his slick skin and his overheated muscles. "Not at all."

He relaxed even more. "Sweet Joy, I never knew sex could be like that."

She closed her eyes, giving herself up to the peace between them. Tomorrow, she'd think. Now, she just wanted to rest against him.

GRAY WOKE UP AROUND five to find himself lying on his side and wrapped around Joy. He had her head against his chest, one arm underneath her neck and the other around her waist. His thigh had worked its way between her legs. He'd even tucked his foot in so his sole was on the back of her calf.

He hated that he had to return to D.C. The last thing in the world he wanted was to leave his woman and get on a plane.

His woman.

Damn, he liked the sound of that.

And maybe he didn't have to go. Maybe he could just stay through her party.

He kissed Joy's shoulder absently and felt her stir against him. The slow-boil arousal he'd woken up with quickly overflowed, flooding his body with heat and need.

Except considering how demanding he'd been the night before, he wasn't sure whether she'd be ready for more of him.

The question was put to rest when she pulled him over on top of her.

He looked down into her face. Her eyes were low-lidded with the remnants of sleep and the beginnings of passion.

He couldn't find words for how lovely she was to him. How the night before she'd taught him about true passion, not the other way around. How she was reaching him on so many levels that she terrified him and amazed him in turns.

All he could do was show her. With his mouth and his hands. His body.

He kissed her slow and easy, parting her lips with his tongue—

The phone rang on the bedside table, about two feet from his ear. He felt like he'd been shot through the head.

Glaring at the damn thing, he said, "Don't worry, I'm not picking up."

It went silent after four rings.

He was lowering his head back down when it started up again.

And then his cell phone went off in the pocket of his suit jacket. And his BlackBerry started bleating on the top of the dresser.

When he got triple-teamed like this, it was because the world was on fire. Someone important had been assassinated. Or died. Or been brought up on charges.

With a vicious curse, he grabbed the cordless off the bedside table while standing up and going for the portables. "What?"

"It's Dellacore. We got a big issue, boss."

Gray stalked over to his suit, pulled out the cell phone and flipped the thing open. "Hold on, Randolf's on the cell. Yeah, Randy? Dell's on the landline, I'll call you back."

He checked the BlackBerry. Another one of his people.

"So who kicked it?" Gray asked. "Or got kicked?"

He left the bedroom, thinking that maybe Joy could go back to sleep.

AS GRAY SHUT THE DOOR behind himself, Joy curled over on her side. She could hear his voice, low and grim, in the other room.

Her body was still warm from what they had started and she thought of the way he'd looked at her just now, right before he'd kissed her. His eyes had had a kind of depth to them she'd never seen before. If she wasn't deluding herself, it had been something close to love.

Was it even possible? But how else could his incredible passion last night be explained? She didn't need to have had a hundred lovers to know that what had passed between them had been beyond good chemistry. Something had changed between them—

The doors opened and Gray strode into the room. "I have to go to Washington right away."

She scrambled upright, holding a sheet over her breasts. "What happened?"

"Nothing you need to worry about." His words were clipped as he headed into the bathroom.

She heard the shower turn on. Less than ten minutes later, he came back into the bedroom and went straight to the closet.

"Gray? Tell me what's going on."

In mere minutes, he emerged fully dressed. His face was impassive, his mouth nothing but a grim line. He paused by the bed.

"I don't know if I'm going to make it to the party." He bent down, eyes boring into hers. He opened his mouth. Shut it. "I will never forget the warmth you showed me last night."

His lips brushed hers. And then he was gone.

An awful numbness stole over her. She pulled more of the sheets and blankets around her body.

Maybe his father had taken ill again. Or there was some kind of emergency.

He would call her, she thought. Later in the day. He always did.

Except when seven o'clock rolled around and she hadn't heard a word, she felt like she'd been totally forgotten.

She'd spent the whole day in the suite, shut off from the outside world. She'd passed the hours refining her drawings, pretending that she was working while she really was just hanging by the phone.

As she finally showered for dinner, she remembered parts of conversations they'd had, words he had spoken.

I've left a lot of women the morning after and never looked back.

You should have saved it for someone who loved you.

You were absolutely right about that Tiffany's charade. I don't want to get married. I'm never going to get married.

I never knew sex could be like that.

Sex, not love, she thought. He'd never said one word about love.

In a bitter rush, she figured she had to give him some credit. He'd known what he was like and he'd fought himself as long as he could, even when she'd thrown herself at him. So none of this was a surprise. Now that he'd had her, he was done.

But maybe—

She stopped herself. He hadn't cared enough to call or even explain why he'd had to leave. Come on, did she really need it spelled out more clearly? She loved him. He didn't love her. That was it.

She forced herself to go down to the Bull and Bear Restaurant and have dinner. As she watched the other patrons laugh and talk over their wine and beef, she was so lonely she wanted to cry.

CHAPTER SIXTEEN

WHEN JOY WALKED OUT onto Fifth Avenue a little after ten the next morning, she felt as if she'd aged a decade for every hour since Gray had taken off without a backward glance.

As she went to her appointments, her sketch folio under her arm, her box of pencils and supplies in her hand, she worked hard to keep from tearing up. To distract herself, she thought of the colors of Saranac Lake. The ice-blue of the autumn sky. The yellow flashes of sunlight over churning, navy waves. The deep green of the hemlock-bearded mountains.

In the midst of the gray, architectural forest she walked through now, she missed the hues and tones of the northern woods.

And the rush of the people around her no longer seemed exciting. The mania was discordant and jarring. She had to fight to keep her portfolio from being kicked out of her arm as pedestrians brushed up against her. When she stepped off the curb without looking, a taxi honked and its driver flipped her off.

By the time five o'clock came around, Joy headed back to the Waldorf, feeling deflated. The evening's reception loomed over her like a tangible obstacle, something she had to surmount or break through.

She checked the Amtrak schedule. The last train

leaving for upstate pulled out of Penn Station at ten forty-five. The party was starting at seven and would be over by nine-thirty. If she packed her things, she'd just have to stop by the hotel to get her bags before she headed across town for the trip home.

As she rode up to Gray's suite in the elevator, she thought that the fantasy of coming to New York, being with a handsome, powerful man and finding success in a career was a good fantasy. But only on paper. The reality had left her bruised, older and painfully wiser.

She would go back to Saranac Lake and complete the five gowns. If tonight yielded any more prospects, she could return to the city if she wanted to, but her home base was going to remain upstate. With the money she'd earned so far, she could afford to move into a small apartment with Grand-Em until White Caps was back in working shape. And she could probably camp out with Alex in their father's workshop until she found a place of her own.

The elevator came to a stop, a bell chiming. She stepped out into the creamy hallway and looked down at the beautiful golds and maroons of the carpet.

One thing was certain. She was never staying at the Waldorf Astoria Hotel ever again, no matter how much cash she had.

"HELLO, DAD," GRAY SAID as he walked into his father's study. He'd been back in Washington since the prior morning, but this was the first chance he'd had to get home. "I know you've heard."

As was now typical, his father was not seated behind the big mahogany desk but was in front of the fire. A red tartan throw covered his legs though the room was warm.

"I. Have."

Gray sat down in the closest chair. He still couldn't believe what had happened, even after having spent the last day and a half talking about the tragedy nonstop with news outlets, political figures, pundits.

John Beckin was dead. Had been found hanging in his bathroom by one of his staff.

"You okay?" Gray asked.

His father frowned. "Sad."

Gray looked away, not wanting his eyes to show.

"Son?" When there was no response, his father leaned forward, taking Gray's hand and shaking it. "Son? Talk."

Gray squeezed his father's palm and then sat back in the chair.

His father cracked his cane into the floor, the sound a demand he didn't have the strength to make with his voice.

Gray cleared his throat. "I saw Becks two nights before he did it. We argued. I, uh—it got nasty. Real nasty."

"Think. Fault. Yours?"

"Hell, Dad. I threatened to expose some of the things he's done."

"No. Fault." His father's head shook back and forth steadily. "Beckin. Been. Threaten. Hundreds. Times."

Yeah, that was no doubt true. But Gray somehow couldn't escape the burden of knowing he'd probably been the last to do it. And both he and Beckin had known he was serious. Unless Beckin had retired, Gray had been prepared to expose him.

There was a long silence.

"Beckin. Was. Talking."

"What, Papa?" Gray sat forward, planting his elbows on his knees, not really hearing what Walter was saying.

"Newspapers."

Gray frowned. "I'm sorry, what?"

"Anna. Shaw. Call. Me. Yesterday." His father took a deep breath, as if the effort of talking was exhausting him, but he was determined to get the words out. "Want. Comment. On. Death."

Gray waited as his father struggled to gather his thoughts and make them come out of his mouth right.

"At. End. I. Said. Will. Miss. Him." There was a pause. "She. Mutter. Yes. Best. Source. She. Ever. Had."

Gray felt shivers cross his skin. "Beckin was the Senate leak?"

His father nodded. "She. Take. Back. Words. So. Probably. True."

Gray leaned back in the chair.

"Don't. Blame. You. Self. Beckin. Demons. Own. Many."

"My God."

His father's head fell back, his eyes closing. He looked so old. So frail.

Gray wondered how much time they had left together.

"I love you," Gray whispered. God, how long had it been since he'd said those words to his father?

Walter's eyes fluttered open. The surprise in them told Gray it had been ages since they'd shared a moment like this. Even after the stroke, Gray had been so busy trying to take care of things, trying to be strong, that he hadn't done a lot of talking.

But that had always been his weakness, hadn't it?

"I love you, Papa," Gray said loudly and clearly.

"Love. You. Son."

"I'll call you later."

"Okay." His father's eyes closed, but his face had eased. There was a peace to him that went beyond the moment, that stretched back into the past and ahead into the future.

As Gray was leaving the room, his assistant called on the cell.

"I've booked you on the shuttle back to New York," she said. "Your plane leaves in forty minutes. You better hustle."

Gray knew he should probably stay in Washington, but the need to get back to Joy was too loud to ignore. Besides, his people would know where to find him and he'd already talked to CNN, FNC and the three major networks. He'd also touched base with his clients who were all nervous about how the death might affect the election. And he'd spent twenty minutes on the phone with the President.

God, he'd wanted to call Joy since he'd left her, but there hadn't been a minute to spare.

And there was more to it than that. She'd rocked his world the night before last and he wanted her to know it, but not over the damn phone. The need to tell her everything, to lay himself bare was what was driving him back to her. As much as he didn't deserve Joy, as much as his feelings scared him, as much as loving her might change him, he had to let her know.

It was almost eight when he landed at JFK and he went straight to the Congress Club. When he walked into the lobby, he could hear the sound of the reception reverberating off the marble walls. Going over to the club's ballroom, he paused in the doorway.

Everything was set up exactly as he'd asked. Joy's designs were posted around on brass standards. There were massive bouquets of fresh flowers. Candles were lit and glowing. And people were crowding to get to the woman in the center of the room.

Joy was wearing a chrome-yellow gown that fit her like water, the swirling beauty of her hair set off by the outrageous color. She was talking with animation, smiling. People were staring at her in awe.

She didn't need him, he thought with pride. She was in control of herself and the room.

He thought back to the night of the barbecue, when she'd danced in his arms. She'd seemed so young to him then, but now he saw her as the woman she was. Strong. Elegant. Smart.

A man walked into the circle surrounding her. When he slipped his arm around her waist, Gray stiffened, but he realized it was just a reflex. As Joy subtly, but firmly, stepped away, he thought that though her unguarded rebuff told him so much, he didn't need the confirmation that she wasn't with anyone else. Not after the night when they'd finally been together.

He was the one with the problem. And he was never going to tangle his past with her integrity again.

"Grayson Bennett, right?"

Gray glanced over his shoulder, frowning. "Do I know you?"

"I'm with the *New York Post.* Here to cover the new designer. But now that I see you, can I get a quote about Beckin's suicide?"

"No, you can't."

"Are you surprised? Do you have any idea what might have caused him to kill himself?"

At that moment, a journalist from the *Times* looked through the crowd at Gray and started making her way over. A couple of other people noticed him and started whispering.

Gray turned and strode out of the lobby. He wasn't going to ruin Joy's moment. As much as he wanted to be in there with her, his presence was going to kick up the Beckin scandal and dilute her exposure.

He'd see her back at the suite.

As Joy stepped away from the man who'd put his arm around her waist, she glanced across the room and caught sight of a dark head turning away at the entrance.

Gray.

Her heart went cold as she watched him leave.

God, even after the night they'd had together, he was still convinced any man who touched her was going home with her.

"Joy? Are you all right?"

She turned and forced a smile at Cassandra. "Yes. I am."

"Well, then come over here and meet Lula Rathbone."

Two hours later the reception wound down and Joy was in a taxi heading back to the Waldorf. She regretted like hell not bringing her bags with her and hoped Gray had gone elsewhere.

When she opened the door to the suite, she listened carefully. Hearing no sound, she rushed into the guest bedroom.

Only to find him sitting in a wing chair. Right next to her luggage.

His hands were up in a bridge in front of his chest. He looked grim.

"You're packed," he said.

"I'm leaving."

"Why?"

"There's a ten forty-five to Albany."

She went over and grabbed the portfolio and her battered suitcase. His hand whipped out, stopping her.

"Let me go," she said.

"I don't want to."

"Why? Do you need to get laid again?"

He hissed, hand tightening. "Is that what you thought our night together was?"

"Yes. I do." Because making love takes two, she thought. And it was just sex to you.

His hand fell away. He seemed to pale, as if he were either shocked or offended.

More likely the latter, she thought.

"You know I suppose I should thank you," she bit out. "You've taught me so much and turned me into a success, just like one of your candidates, right? You told me what to wear and what to say, and you got the players all lined up, and everything went smoothly. They loved my work and I'm sure I'll be getting more clients so I guess I have a steady job now. It's a hell of a payback you gave me for just a couple of hours with my body."

Gray rose from the chair, fury in his face. "You think I'm that kind of man?"

"You don't love me. You don't trust me. But you're clearly susceptible to guilt. Tonight was just a different version of that showdown at Tiffany's. I figure now you think you can walk away with a clean conscience."

He loomed over her, enraged. "Just so you know, I had no intention of walking away from you. Until now." He marched around her, heading into the living room. "Don't let the door hit you on the ass when you leave, sweetheart."

As if he were the one who'd been wronged.

She went after him, lugging her stuff. "You have a hell of a nerve getting pissed off! You're the one who walked out on me two days ago."

"Are you still here?" he drawled from the bar as he poured himself a bourbon. When he turned to her, his stare was icy.

Looking up at him, she felt tears prick the corners of her eyes.

"Oh, good. Now you're going to cry," he snapped. "You insult the hell out of me, get all huffy because I'm offended, and then pull the weepy routine. I never pictured you as a gamer, but maybe I was wrong. You want me to get all romantic and beg you to stay now, right?"

"No, I would never expect that," she whispered.

"What a relief."

"Because you are incapable of love."

His eyes narrowed. "How the hell would you know what I'm—"

"Have I ever done anything to betray you?"

"Excuse me?"

"Tonight, at the reception. I saw you turn away when that man came up to me. Even after all this time, you still think I'm going to run off with any idiot in pants who looks my way. In fact, I'm willing to bet you think Tom's going to be my first stop when I get up north, don't you? You probably figure I'm going to try out all those moves you taught me in your bed, right?" He opened his mouth, but she kept going. "God, I must have done something really awful to you, although I can't even begin to guess what it was. You don't even trust me enough to talk about your work."

"What does my job have to do with this?"

"Every time I brought up what you do, you pushed me away."

"You don't want to know about—"

"I did. I truly did. When you came up to White Caps that night and you finally spoke to me about something in your life, I was so relieved. I thought, See, he does view me as an equal. He does trust me. But then you pulled away, shut the door, closed up." She shook her head. "This has been one wild ride. I've loved you for years and the only thing that lived up to my expectations was the way you felt inside of me two nights ago. But like all dreams, that went away when I woke up."

"You've loved me for years?" he said softly.

She looked away from his face, unable to bear the sight of him.

"Yeah, stupid, isn't it? And here's the craziest part. When I said those words that first night we were together, guess what? I really meant them." She laughed harshly. "But don't worry, I'm over it. I might be dumb enough to get caught in a fantasy, but I'm not a masochist." She jacked up her load. "So goodbye, Gray. It's been real. Way, way too real. Oh, one more thing. I know one-nighters are your specialty, but in case you get an itch up north and start thinking of coming to find me, don't. I don't want to ever see you again."

She turned around and strode across the carpet. As she left the suite, the door closed of its own volition behind her.

PENN STATION WAS FAIRLY BUSY even though it was late and Joy got a lot of funny looks as she sped along with her luggage. Even in New York, evidently, the sight of a woman in a chrome-yellow evening gown steaming through a mass transit lobby was a curiosity.

Her train was already waiting so she hiked up her dress and hightailed it down to the platform. At the far end of the line of cars, way in front by the engine, there was a uniformed ticket collector and he waved her over to him.

"You need help with all that, ma'am?" he asked as she approached.

"No, I'm fine. Thanks."

"Here, lemme get you on board." He took her suitcase and gave her a hand up.

His casual politeness nearly undid her and he seemed surprised when her eyes welled, as if women who wore evening gowns never cried.

Stepping into the railcar, she saw there were plenty of seats available. She took one by the window, shuffling her portfolio and suitcase into the space on the floor with the porter's help. She eyed the bathroom, which was only four rows away. Tissues were going to play an important role on the trip home and it was good to know she was close to a ready supply.

With a whistle and a lurch, the train started to move.

She leaned her head back and closed her eyes. Sure enough, the tears started to fall.

Dimly, from the platform, she heard some shouting, but she ignored the commotion as the line of cars sped up, the engine in front chugging, churning, gaining momentum as it took them toward the tunnel.

When the cars were going at quite a clip, someone said, "My God, he's going to jump!"

Joy glanced behind her. People had stopped trying to settle their carry-ons and were looking out the windows. With little interest, she turned to the glass.

There was a man running by the side of the train, tie flapping behind him. He was yelling something.

My God, was it—

"Gray?"

She shot out of her seat. Just as he took a leap into the air.

"Gray!" she screamed.

FEET DON'T FAIL ME NOW, Gray thought as he hurled his body toward the open doorway of the last car.

In midair, he eyed the train wheels below and then glanced up at the fast-approaching entrance to the tunnel.

Now there were two great choices. Sliced in half or flat as a pancake.

Fortunately his trajectory and speed had been right, but as he sailed through the doorway, the leather soles of his wing tips slid on the metal flooring. He grabbed onto a hand bar to keep from shooting out the other side.

As soon as he had his footing, he started running down the aisle, scanning the passengers. People leaped out of his way, magazines flying, pocketbooks exploding from hands, luggage being dropped.

Far, far down the way, through the open doors of many cars, he saw Joy's bright yellow dress. She was jumping out of her seat, looking at him with horror.

"We're not finished," he shouted, tearing down the train toward her. "Joy! We're not finished, you and I!"

When he finally reached her, he careened to a stop, panting for breath, holding on to the top of seats to steady himself.

"We're…not…finished."

"Are you trying to get yourself killed!"

A porter came up to them. "Sir, I'm going to have to—"

Gray shoved his hand into his pocket. "Here's… my…ticket."

The porter looked at the thing as if it might have been in a different language. Clearly, the guy hadn't seen too many passengers board on a wing and a prayer.

"Excuse me, ma'am," the porter said. "Is this man bothering you? Ma'am?"

Joy shook her head, but more as if she were mourning Gray's lack of mental health than answering the guy's question. She opened her mouth.

"I love you," Gray said.

Her face shot up to his, her lovely hair spilling back. "What?"

"I love you! Joy Moorehouse, I love you!" he bellowed.

Joy stared at him. And so did the woman sitting in the row of seats behind her. And the man across the aisle. Actually, pretty much all of the people on the train were focused on him.

The porter smiled. "Um, ma'am?"

"No, he's not bothering me. But he's nuts." She grabbed Gray's arm and tugged him down so they were sitting together. "What are you—"

He took her face into his hands and kissed her fiercely. "I love you. And I'm praying that I'm not too late."

She pulled back, dazed. "I don't understand."

He took her hands in his and squeezed. "How long is this train ride?"

"Uh, three hours."

"Good. I've got a lot of talking I need to do."

BY THE TIME THEY WERE just outside of Albany, Joy stopped believing it was a dream. Gray told her about everything. His mother. His father. His childhood.

"And that's why, the night I drove up to see you," he said, "I pulled away like I did. I promised myself that I'd never be like Papa, but there I was, traveling three hundred miles out of my way, just to see you. Even though I knew you weren't like my mother, I got burned so badly trying to keep my parents together that letting myself go, letting myself fall for you, it just didn't feel safe. I panicked."

He stroked her hair, his eyes tender. "Joy, I'm sorry. I'm sorry I put you through hell and that it took me so long to get my act together. You've never done one thing to justify my mistrust." He took a deep breath and dragged his hand through his hair. He'd been doing that a lot and now the dark waves were sticking up willy-nilly, at odds with his tailored, sophisticated clothes. "After you left the suite tonight, I felt like I had a chest wound, I hurt so badly, and I just couldn't let you leave without at least telling you how I felt. Look, I'll understand if you've had it with me. I wouldn't blame you. I've handled this relationship with a total lack of…finesse. Common sense. Hell, good manners. And you know what the irony is? I started out thinking I was too old for you. That's wrong. In a lot of ways, you're the mature one. You know how you feel. You can talk about your emotions. I'm a mess in that department. But...God...I...I love you."

Gray stopped speaking and looked down at their hands. He'd held on to her the entire time he'd spoken and now, in his silence, he was as vulnerable as she'd ever seen him. His eyes were raw, worried, even though she had the sense he was trying to hide his desperation.

"I need to know," he said softly. "Is it too late? Have I blown it?"

She put her fingertip under his chin and lifted his face up. Leaning forward, she pressed her lips to his and watched as his eyes flared.

"No, you're not too late."

His arms shot around her, crushing her against his chest until she couldn't breathe. When he finally loosened his hold, she heard a sniffle and craned her neck around. The woman in the seat behind them was wiping her eyes, a sappy smile on her face.

"Now, about my job," Gray said, growing grim again. "I've done some things I'm not...proud of. I didn't want to talk about work with you because I hated being reminded of them. And frankly, I didn't want you to know."

In halting, slow words, he talked about John Beckin's death and the role he believed he might have played in it. His sadness, his self-blame were hard to see.

"Oh, Gray." She stroked his hand.

"Listen, I've got to be honest. I need to get out of politics. I can't do it anymore. I've been disenchanted with the whole scene for a couple of years, but now, after what happened with Beckin, I just—I can't do this. I can't..." He shook his head. "I can't do this. Which means, you understand, that I'm not going to be some big, powerful guy anymore. The President's not going to be calling me. I'm not going to be hanging with the country's leaders. I'm just going to be a regular schmoe—"

She put her hand over his mouth.

"No offense, Gray. But shut up." She smiled gently. "Do you honestly think any of that matters to me? I'll take you any way I can have you. And I'm glad you're getting out. If your work was making you that unhappy, if it was making you do things you hated yourself for, then you need to be somewhere else."

"But you deserve a man who's—"

"By my side and happy in his life."

He fell silent. "You know, maybe I can teach more at Columbia. I think I'd like being a full-time professor." He shrugged. "But who knows. Look, I've got to warn you, you're marrying an unemployed man, here."

"Marrying? Marrying?" she stuttered.

He smiled. "Come on, you don't think I'm ever going to let you go now, do you? I'm an old-fashioned kind of guy. I want to be married to my woman. And I want to be her husband. Your husband."

She stared at him. "You said you weren't ever going to get—"

He kissed her. "I was wrong."

Gray shifted his legs around and stood up. With steady hands, he straightened his tie and jacket.

And then in front of a carload of breathless strangers, he got down on one knee in the aisle.

"I don't have a ring, but I can't wait any longer. Joy, will you be my wife?"

As Joy clapped her hand over her mouth and started to blink fiercely, the woman sitting behind them poked her head around the seat. "Honey, if you don't marry him, I'm gonna."

Joy laughed and looked at the other passenger. "Sorry, but I think I'll take him up on the offer."

"Damn. I figured you might." The woman winked and disappeared back into her seat.

"So, will you?" Gray asked. "Even though I haven't done a damn thing right since we started seeing each other and even though I'm a pigheaded son of a bitch sometimes? I promise I'll always love you. And I'll always take care of you. And I'll—"

"Shh." Joy leaned over, stroking his eyebrows and his cheeks with her thumbs. God, she loved his face, his harsh, arrogant, beautiful face. She kissed his forehead and then his mouth. "Yes. I will marry you."

In a joyous rush, the sound of clapping rippled through the car. She looked up in surprise. As the train rolled to a stop at the Albany station, the other passengers stood and cheered.

While Gray stared up at her, his pale eyes shining through dark lashes, Joy couldn't believe what had happened. What was happening.

"Pinch me," she whispered.

"What?"

"So I know this is real."

Gray smiled, and pulled her down to his mouth. "How about I kiss you again, instead?"

"Even better."

* * * * *